CONSCIOUSNESS
(with *Mutilation*)

By Anthony Howell

ODD VOLUMES

OF

THE FORTNIGHTLY REVIEW

LES BROUZILS

2019

*Consciousness (*with *Mutilation) is* a non-fiction novel. Every sentence that begins any paragraph within it also serves as the concluding sentence of another paragraph. The trigger for the text is an epileptic seizure the author experienced in April 2018. This event prompted an investigation of the meaning of continuity in individuals, families and states. Could we have been somebody else yesterday, or become somebody else tomorrow? Consciousness annexes a Syrian novella – *Mutilation* – within its pages. *Mutilation* is a novella by Mamdouh Adwan, first published in Damascus in 1971. Reading this book is to be drawn into whirlpools, perhaps to drown. It is self-analysis, but, since the author's lineage is both Jewish and Quaker, it evolves into an analysis of Zionism, of which Howell's grandfather was a proponent, and of the role of the British in the Middle East. Having experienced sudden lapses of consciousness, the author senses that "life is not a river. Life is a collage."

By Anthony Howell

POETRY
Inside the Castle 1969
Imruil 1970
Oslo: a Tantric Ode 1975
Notions of a Mirror 1983
Why I May Never See the Walls of China 1986
Howell's Law 1990
First Time in Japan 1995
Sonnets 1999
Selected Poems 2000
Spending 2000
Dancers in Daylight 2003
Statius: Silvae *(with Bill Shepherd)* 2007
The Ogre's Wife 2009
Plague Lands *(versions of Fawzi Karim)* 2011
The Empty Quarter *(versions of Fawzi Karim)* 2014
Silent Highway 2014
Poems of Alain-Fournier
(with Anthony Costello and Anita Marsh) 2017
From Inside 2017

FICTION
In the Company of Others 1986
Oblivion 2002

PROSE
Elements of Performance Art *(with Fiona Templeton)* 1976
The Analysis of Performance Art 1999
Serbian Sturgeon 2000/2018

AS EDITOR
Near Calvary: The Selected Poems of Nicholas Lafitte 1992

The novella *Mutilation* by Mamdouh Adwan in a new version by Anthony Howell is included in these pages by courtesy of Adwan Publishing, Damascus.

To the memory of Razan al-Najjar

Odd Volumes
The Fortnightly Review

Editorial office: Château le Ligny
2 rue Georges Clémenceau 85260 Les Brouzils France.

http://fortnightlyreview.co.uk/odd-volumes/

email info@fortnightlyreview.co.uk

Photographs: Nimrod (1939) by Itzhak Danziger.
Gift of Dr. David H. Orgler, Zurich and Jerusalem,
The Israel Museum, Jerusalem.

ISBN: 978-0-9991365-3-9

Author's note:

This book takes *The Naked Lunch* by William Burroughs and *Jealousy* by Alain Robbe-Grillet for its literary forbears. In the way of ancient tragedy, the dilemma of the individual becomes the dilemma of the state, in this case Israel, and the author carries the reader into a world of smoke and mirrors, sustained by collage mediated through its formal constraint.
— Anthony Howell

My horse goes hell-for-leather across the common. In point of fact, Steeldust is a pony, not a horse. He's thirteen/two. He used to be a polo pony. That was how he was trained. It means you can guide him with only one hand, and he'll follow the lead from the pressure on his neck on the other side to that in which one wishes to turn. This is so that you can swing your polo mallet with the other hand. Steeldust is a wonder at dressage. When we do dressage, I feel that I am dancing with my mount. We can do turns on the foreleg, sidesteps, changes of leg or flying changes. I could be dancing the tango. Like dressage, the tango is all lead and follow. At the age of thirteen, I was a dab hand at dressage. At the age of seventy-three, I am a tanguero. I go to sleep as the one, and wake up as the other. In both cases, there is this sense of oneness incorporated into being a couple. Horse and Man. Boy and pony rather. Leader and follower. Man and woman rather. What the man instigates by invitation, the woman completes, just as the pony completes the lead from the thigh. The aids that comprise the lead. The lead that originates here in the sternum. Man and beast. Man and woman. We can be so together. As much a part of a single entity as are yin and yang. Or I can be bucked off. It's happened more than once to me. Or she can come at me, fierce, hostile as a lioness; the fingers there in my face to scratch my eyes out. Fuck, you fucking bastard! Don't give me that, you bitch! These are the states we go through. Some we delight in, some we survive, some we don't survive. Out of the chrysalis of the victim, a monster emerges. But also, out of the strong, may come forth a sweetness. Wasn't that the image you saw on tins of Tate and Lyle? The bees who built their honeycomb in the entrails of the lion's corpse. As a species, our anomalies are confusing for all of us. We like to divide ourselves into innocents and criminals, but we all know our own criminal acts. Even if nobody else does. We are troglodytes and bonobos at the same time, rather than two distinct species. And we like to think of ourselves as distinct. For instance, I like to imagine that I am a man, and that I have always been of the male sex, even when I was a boy. But how do I know for sure that this is the case? In every aspect, life inflicts changes upon us. Homeostasis implies that sometimes I lack something and sometimes I am carrying around some surplus or excess. Balance cannot be a steady state. The drum that creates is matched by the fire that destroys. As a suckling infant, I am utterly engaged in being in a state of hunger, and then, when I'm replete, I'm in another state altogether. Later, in puberty perhaps, God, I am feeling so horny, and this influences everything I do, everything I think, and then I have sex or I wank and I come or I ejaculate, and I'm in a post-horny state. One state gets collaged against another. Life itself is a collage of dreams and realities. No one can remain uninterruptedly awake. Only death allows us to sleep forever, or so we suppose, or so we may suppose. And though we may feel possessive about our identities, can we be sure that we've always been ourselves? For instance, all I know about myself is that I am sitting here, experiencing the touch of the keys on my fingertips and watching my writing emerge on the screen in front of my eyes. Here, in this present moment, I can recall being seated on Dusty. Getting him to pivot on his right forehoof, or going hell-for-leather across the common with Katie and the palomino not so far behind me. I know this in the present as I feel the keys beneath my fingertips. Pretty soon, I'll feel sleepy. I am one for cat-naps and siestas. Pretty soon I'll fall asleep. Will I be me, when I wake up? The inevitable break in continuity insists upon my acknowledging that I can never be sure. When I wake up how do I know who I was when I went to sleep?

"That's my Ribena." I must have felt possessive about that. I'd bought the small plastic bottle of Ribena upstairs in the forecourt of Saint Pancras Station, before walking through the barrier onto the Kings Cross platform I needed to get up to Leeds, while on my way to Huddersfield, my destination. After the seizure, I never saw it again, that bottle of Ribena. I don't deal with loss terribly well. I was sent to a psychiatrist at the age of seven or eight, because I was having trouble with arithmetic. I simply couldn't subtract. I feel guilty about things that have been stolen from me. Recently, I wrote a poem about my losses:

> That crystal goblet – it had stood on my mother's bedroom
> Chest-of-drawers for ever, as Brigid had, her wooden cow
> Kept since she was a child, head chewed by a dog though,
> Body daubed with big red spots; gone, as have the Arnesby Browns:
> The small one of the windmill, last seen in a storm across a field
> Of corn, the larger one of cows in a sun-fumed pasture.

> Gone, gone, as have the zoological volumes, ages old,
> Illustrated with wood-cuts, the Senna kilim taken from my
> Flat in Islington, the cricket bat with autographs of Hobbs and

The rest of the team, given me by Uncle Paul, who must
Have gone up and asked for them at the end of some long
Afternoon at Lords. Gone, along with his father's Sandhurst

Sword of honour. Stolen, lost, or simply forgotten.
Absences that lose me sleep, as does that magnificent oak
Felled by some farmer who begrudged the shade it cast on his crop.
Not the death of my father, since that is simply an idea:
He had been killed before I was born, so never someone
Missed the way I missed my intellectual cousin Jean,

Found collapsed on the floor of her flat, and Clemency
Who stole my heart without intending it. She phoned me up
Years later, after I was married, then committed suicide,
As Nick did, as did Graham; and my tiny daughter Storm
Who crawled away delighted by my chasing her and then was gone,
Gone like the ball I watched at four float away down the Hudson.

As a researcher into mastitis, my mother had a lot to do with cows, and I am glad that when the wonderful painting by Arnesby Brown of cows grazing in the haze of summer was stolen from her Powys farm, she was already too far gone with dementia to take much interest in the loss. I felt guilty about not having taken the painting into my own self-keeping before that raid on the farm, and I have to confess also that I feel, or at least I felt, a little guilty about stealing from my mother between the ages of seven and twelve. At the time, I assumed my mother never noticed. I stole larger and larger amounts. I spent most of the money buying guns or soldiers. I amassed Colts and Lugers. I horded my weaponry, taking it into school in a large shoul-der-bag with a zip – to impress the other boys. Why did I need to impress them so much? I ended up purchasing an air-pistol modelled into a revolver that came in an authentic leather holster. I got it out only with my most trusted friends. This was my one and only serious weapon. It could have taken out an eye. I hid the gun in the bushes along the drive down to the garage. One day it was gone. I couldn't tell anyone. A, it was dangerous and B, I had stolen the cash to buy it. Who stole the gun out of those bushes? Who stole the sword of honour? Had the revolver been stolen by someone I knew? One of the boys I trusted because we would get out our penises in my grandmother's room, upstairs, at the far end of the cottage. It was vacant most of the time, only occupied when my grandmother came down to Reading from London to visit us. In point of fact, I think I am eliding things here. I stole guns to show to my prep school friends. I got my penis out to share it with one or other of the boys in my class at the public school where I was a day-boarder, by which time the revolver had been stolen and I had given up theft in disgust and had started to ejaculate instead. Is burglary the longing for a home? Sometimes, I have been told, burglars, especially young ones, break in and shit on other people's carpets. But when Fay found me, back when? A year ago? There was shit all over the carpet. So had I shat in my own home? How fucking psychological is that? Did I burgle my own house? What the hell does that amount to? What does a seizure mean? But now I am way off track. I had been meaning to expand upon why I feel so guilty when things are stolen from me. My guilt then is far worse than when I am the one who is doing the stealing. When I was the one. It is far more inevitable, I feel, to blame oneself for a theft suffered than for a theft perpetrated. Now I feel so guilty about the sword.

"Where am I?" That's what I've kept on saying, I'm told, when I come to. I find myself sitting on the back of a horse, as twilight darkens around us. It feels just like a dream. Just like it does when I find myself horizontal in an ambulance, watching the tall trees on either side of the road disappear behind us through the double windows in the rear doors. Who am I? Am I Julia Skripal? Have I been assassinated? Still groggy from it all, I posted my suspicion on Facebook. For the record, this is all happening in 2018, not more than a month after the Skripals have been found unconscious in Salisbury. Becca made a comment on my post. Quite a while ago, she used to be my girlfriend. We went to the Algarve together. We swam in the sea and I painted water-colours of her - some of which she may have found unflattering. We watched eagles circling above distant crags. Becca saw my recent post and said she hardly thought Mossad would consider me important enough to assassinate. I used to come up to Leeds to visit her – on the same express.

"Can I keep my chips?" That's what I remember saying when I came to on the ground beneath dark trees, a hundred yards from the chip shop on the Old Kent Road. It is strange how vividly one remembers being knocked out. The before, and the after, at least. But between the before and the after, well, there is nothing. That is so different to dreams. With dreams, you find yourself completely within some narrative while the wakeful state before is just not there, and of course, neither is the state you will wake up in, sometime in some future perhaps… Perhaps… In the dream, while you're involved in it, you simply can't be sure. Not while meeting the editor in Germany for lunch. At the tavern he has suggested, you find him engaged in playing some game chalked on the paving stones of the courtyard. He greets you warmly enough when you arrive, but then someone who worked on a film which is showing tells you both that it's against the law to change anything in the film after the final cut, so your mistake will have to stay as it is. You try to point out that your mistake happens in the penultimate paragraph, after the film has concluded, not while it's actually playing, but nobody listens, and the editor hands you a joint wrapped, not in paper, but in unleavened bread. You are squatting by the paving stones with him where the game has been chalked, but others have rejected this joint, saying it seems like it has been totally inside other people's mouths, though the editor explains that the waitress has explained to him that it's because the dough was still wet when the joint was rolled. You take a somewhat distasteful toke, just as the judge walks by, glancing your way. It is clear he disapproves, though the editor (who you have never met in real life) looks up at him with a friendly smile. You realise that the judge's disapproval is not directed at your stupid mistake but at the sogginess of the joint you are attempting without much success to inhale. It must be strong, because the next thing you know you are trimming everyone's hair at the same time as you are cooking them pork chops. After that, you get employed to take people to a fund-raising party on a barge. You feel that this is a dream that your grand-father ought to be having instead of you. But do I mean you, or do I mean me, or do I mean Julia Skripal? Any which way, I am pretty sure that they have tried bumping her off, or you or me. Why else should I have had that bruised puncture between the middle finger and the second finger of my right hand? Perhaps they were practising their assassination technique on me.

You have to be well enough to write about sickness. For the first fortnight after the seizures, I could do nothing but lie in bed, either asleep or exhausted, staggering to the bathroom, permanently suffering from the shits. One day I set out on a journey up to Huddersfield as a poet, and then there was this ambulance, and then, well, I conked out again, I guess, and then, there is a hospital bed, and what am I? I'm in nappies, that's what I am. And once, as a boy of ten, I reached up to pluck an orange off the bough of an orange tree. This was in a kibbutz which seemed like the Garden of Eden to me. No one minds what time I turn off the light, so I stay up, reading my Uncle's copy of *Brave New World.* My cousin Jonah lives on this kibbutz. He's friendly with his neighbours, his Arab neighbours in the village just next to the kibbutz. This is in 56. Some fifteen years later, he won't speak to the Arabs. I guess one of his comrades on the kibbutz or on a neighbouring kibbutz got shot. At the time that I heard about how much his attitude had changed, I supposed that the shooter must have been a fellaheen countryman, seething with revenge against these Zionist settlers. Now, I am not as convinced about this as I was. There is more smoke and there are more mirrors in the world I exist in today. These days I suspect Mossad of shooting those kibbutzniks. One night, a nation went to sleep as a democracy, and the next morning it woke as a fascist regime.

Did the rails electrocute my brain? I remember feeling the speed. Not in myself, since I was completely stationary, but I felt it in the way a platform of some rural station will flash by in an instant. In the dragon strength of the power beneath my seat. I think of Shiva at Seven Sisters. There, they have demolished the old three storey Apex building. And a twenty-three-storey lift-shaft has risen like a minaret, high up into the sky. The sheer power of the modern is something I find increasingly daunting. The speed of modern movement, the speed of erection. When my Grandfather went to school in Germany, back in the nineteenth century, he went with the other children in a horse-drawn bus. Every two miles, a man in a hut extended a stick with a leather pouch on the end of it, and into this pouch a few pfennigs were deposited by the driver. I think of Shiva at Seven Sisters, which is where I go down into the underground when making my way to Kings Cross, because the developer is always a destroyer. 23 floors, 36 floors, and upwards. 50 miles per hour, 80 miles per hour, 110 miles per hour and upwards. And construction must demolish whatever was there before; which in turn demolished what was there before that. So rather than a continuity of time, our world has got where it is today by dint of discontinuity. Is this discontinuity universal? Do we even wake up as the person we were before we went to sleep? Maybe tomorrow I will wake up as my father, or as my Uncle Paul.

I ended up in the Acute Assessment Unit. Hinchinbrook Hospital. I must have either wet myself or shat myself, since I was clad in nappies. My damp jeans were draped over the back of a chair. At least I knew where I had been going. I managed to get a nurse to deliver a message to the Square Chapel in Halifax, where I was due to read. I had no mobile with me. I haven't got used to mobiles. But that name, the "Square Chapel" had stuck in my mind. Luckily. Was it a square chapel or a chapel in a square? I have to say, this was not the most urgent of the questions presented to my consciousness as I came to in nappies on that April day. Later, after a display of considerable hysterics, I managed to get an appointment in London with the specialist I had seen a year before, after an incident in my home that had not actually been witnessed by anyone, only supposed by Fay, when she came in to find me sprawled on the bed and faeces on the study carpet. She had insisted that I got to see a specialist. She took me there in her car, when this first appointment came up, and her account of what had occurred that afternoon differed radically from

mine. This led to an MRI scan. At the time, I kept on contradict-
ing her as we sat in front of the doctor. Today I am not so sure that
my account was correct and hers incorrect. Seizures are disorienting
incidents. But perhaps all lapses of consciousness, even dropping off
for a nap, are just as liable to disorientation. After all, after I had knelt
under the table to retrieve my spectacles, which had fallen to the
floor of this stationary yet still convulsively shuddering train taking
me up to Huddersfield, where Keith was to meet me and drive me to
the Halifax reading – after all, I decided, settling back into my seat,
after a sip of my Ribena, not to read, no, but to lean my head against
the carriage's window-frame, in order to take a nap on this Reality
TV show. I think I'm supposed to be the anchor. There is a wager,
which is, whether a tennis star who is also a damn good jockey can
ride from Volgograd to the clinic in London before JLo and Andy
Murray can have a baby. The bets are placed, and the competition
begins as soon as JLo goes into labour. I've been invited to participate
because whoever wins gets to host Poetry at The Room with me. I
don't properly grasp what it's all about, meanwhile I am distracted by
watching Navratilova mounting the horse on TV, lots of struggling
to get the horse on her feet and started, then we switch to watching
JLo give birth – outflow a dam-burst – while Andy uses some sort
of fret-saw to sever the incredibly tough umbilical cord. The baby
just comes out first, though it is something of a photo finish, and I
rush off to tell all my friends that JLo will be hosting Poetry at The
Room. However, Holcombe Road has become a synagogue in the
wee small hours of the 2nd of July. We are back there now, performing Judaic ceremonies which involve bathing in baths of appropri-
ated tahina or humous, but at the same time we are critiquing these
ceremonies, getting them wrong, deliberately pouring scorn on their
sacred functions with our own hostile reactions as murmuring is

heard from the garden. The police have informed on us, and angry forces are gathering, vengeful forces. Desperately, I struggle to draw the curtains, which are always a problem, trying to seal us off from the outer world. Clearly, sleep is as crammed with incident as any wakeful day. Wakeful days such as yesterday, or the day when Fay discovers me sprawled out on the bed. How can she tell whether I'm unconscious or asleep? And what about today? Is Fay still Fay? Am I still myself? But I should get a grip. Shake myself free of these doubts about continuity. Doubts that beset Descartes, it has to be said, who also recognised that only a life without sleep could guarantee that we remained whoever we were from the day of our birth to the day of our demise. But doesn't the bible exist to narrate, ever so staunchly, the continuity of the promise? That promise made first to the Neanderthals, and then to Abraham, and then, later, to Moses, and then to Theodor Herzl and now to Benjamin Netanyahu. A continuity as evident as that of the River Jordan, emanating from its sources among the waterfalls of Mount Hermon in the Anti-Lebanon mountain range down through the lake of Galilee and then flowing out of that, down further, below sea-level, to terminate in the Dead Sea. This is a river that has occupied a rift that is part of a continuous geographic trench, approximately 6,000 kilometres in length, which becomes the Great Rift Valley and then the East African Rift that culminates in Mozambique. That name, 'the Great Rift Valley', continues in some usages, although it is today considered geologically imprecise as it combines features that are now regarded as separate, although related, rift and fault systems. Whether separate or not, in its origins, the rift has been the route for thousands of years for hundreds of emigrations. The Jordan runs contrariwise to the exodus from Egypt and in prehistoric times, from Africa – as in not so prehistoric times. It is this continuity that has inspired Rebecca to leave her home among Orthodox parents in Boston, Massachusetts. She used to be plump and awkward. Now she is tough and toned. She emigrated to Israel six years ago. Today she's a trained fighter in IDF intelligence, defending the home she knows and loves.

As I see it, an attempt has been made to assassinate me. So I wonder whether that jolly, rather plump, red-haired lady sitting next to me will end up as a prime-minister. Consider the killing of Count Folke Bernadotte, the UN diplomat and negotiator, on the 17 September 1948 by the Zionist terrorist group, Lehi. Lehi were linked to the Stern gang. A four-man team ambushed Bernadotte's motorcade in Jerusalem's Katamon neighborhood, centred around a Greek Orthodox monastery and in those days haemorrhaging Christians as the trouble worsened. The team left a Lehi base in a jeep, set up a makeshift roadblock, and then waited in the jeep. When Berna- dotte's motorcade approached, three men got out and approached it while the driver remained in the jeep. The motorcade's Israeli liaison officer, who was sitting in the leading UN vehicle, called out in Hebrew to let them through, but was ignored. One man came up to Bernadotte's sedan and fired through an open window, hitting Bernadotte and a French officer who was sitting beside him, Colonel André Serot. Both Bernadotte and Serot were killed. The killing was approved by the three-man 'centre' of Lehi, : Nathan Friedmann, Yisrael Eldad and Yitzhak Yezernitsky (the future Prime Minister Yitzhak Shamir). Bernadotte, unanimously chosen to be the U.N. Security Council mediator in the Arab–Israeli conflict that had been raging between 47 and 48, had proposed two independent states and is on record as having said: 'It is ... undeniable that no settlement can be just and complete if recognition is not accorded to the right of the Arab refugee to return to the home from which he has been dislodged by the hazards and strategy of the armed conflict between Arabs and Jews in Palestine.' This leads me on now to consider the career of Ayad Allawi. While exiled to the UK and still recovering in hospital from a night-time axe attack in his home, Allawi, a Shia Muslim who had also once been a Baathist, started organising an opposition network to work against Saddam. Through the 80s, he built up this network, recruiting Shia Iraqis while traveling as a businessman. In December 1990, Allawi announced the existence of the Iraqi National Accord (the INA). Saddam's largely Sunni government claimed that this organisation orchestrated attacks that caused up to 100 civilian deaths though there are no records of these statistics to be found. It was the INA that channelled the report from an Iraqi officer to British Intelligence claiming that Iraq could deploy its supposed weapons of mass destruction within "45 minutes". I have always thought it likely that Allawi and his INA, intent on installing a Shia government in Iraq, had more reason than anyone to engineer the death of Dr David Kelly, our biological weapons expert who was quoted in *The Observer* as saying, 'They are not mobile germ warfare laboratories. You could not use them for making biological weapons. They do not even look like them. They are exactly what the Iraqis said they were – facilities for the production of hydrogen gas to fill balloons.' After the Second Gulf War, Ayad Allawi became Prime Minister of Iraq. And we've all seen how it has not been so difficult for prominent members of the IRA to become distinguished politicians. That is the way of things. I'm looking forward to seeing a plump, red-haired, rather jolly lady succeed Benjamin Netanyahu. Meanwhile I should be more circumspect when it comes to airing my views in the poetry that I post on Facebook. Now I feel pretty sure it could get me killed. So perhaps it was silly of me to mention the name of Sergei Skripal in my poem entitled *Semper Occultus*. That's the motto of the UK secret service. It was after I had written this poem that the episode occurred.

"The train ahead has hit an object on the line." We had come to a shuddering stop, although the train had not ceased to shudder, to quiver. Vividly in my body, I experienced the sensation of there being electricity everywhere. This was an external sensation, not an internal one. I have felt electric within, as when my performance company, The Theatre of Mistakes, returned elated from a hugely successful European tour. Having dropped everybody off, I parked the VW van that had taken us all to Belgium and back. Applause everywhere. I kept smiling to myself. That was a job well done! I was feeling jaunty in my snarky pin-stripe suit.

It seems only yesterday that I was Martin Rosenbluth, preparing for the evening's meeting, and discussing current affairs and our Zionist predicament with someone who became a lifelong friend and colleague, Nahum Goldmann. In the period 1916-18, Nahum had worked for the German *Nachrichtenstelle für den Orient*, an intelligence and propaganda bureau related to the German Foreign Office, which tried to instrumentalize ethnic and religious nationalist currents within the Ottoman Empire, such as Islamism and Zionism, for German interests; to fight back increasing British and French influence in the region. The Ottoman empire had abandoned its multicultural tolerance for a pan-Turkish policy that infuriated the Arabs under their rule. Nahum talked about a British liaison officer T. E. Lawrence who advised the Bedouin and formed them into effective guerrilla combat units. The political intrigues surrounding the revolt and its aftermath were as significant as the fighting, for Great Britain and France's myopic attempts at nation building kept planting the seeds of the troubles that could plague our chosen region for the foreseeable future: regional conflicts, authoritarian governments, coups, the rise of militant Islam, and the possibility of enduring conflict between our Israeli settlers and their neighbours. "We must always distinguish between propaganda and the news," Nahum pointed out to me. "The job of the propagandist is more akin to that of the advertising copywriter than to that of the journalist. We should not seek to convince simply by sticking to the facts. Sometimes the facts must be played down, and a quiet diplomacy behind the scenes preferred as the more effective means of pursuing our viable goals; at other times, the facts should be exaggerated, six thousand deaths should become sixty thousand or six million even, just as the characteristics of baked beans may be improved by their advertiser, and their number increased beyond the number that can be fitted inside a single tin." "It sounds somehow the opposite of Abraham's compact with God," I remarked. "You remember how, after the angels received the hospitality of Abraham and Sarah, The Lord revealed to Abraham that he would confirm what he had heard against Sodom and Gomorrah, and because their sin was grievous he would consume these cities with fire and brimstone. And then, as I recall, Abraham inquired of the Lord if he would spare the city if fifty righteous people were found in it, to which the Lord agreed he would not destroy it for the sake of the righteous yet dwelling therein. Abraham then inquired of God for mercy at lower numbers: first forty-five, then forty, then thirty, then twenty and finally ten, with the Lord agreeing each time. That is the case, Nahum agreed, "but then what happened?" He asked, making the question rhetorical by continuing, "according to the slant the tale is given, two journalist angels were sent to Sodom to investigate and were met by Abraham's nephew Lot, who convinced the angels to lodge with him, and they ate with Lot, but then there was a commotion outside the door, and according to their report, the townsfolk wanted to break down the door and *know* them, in the worst possible way. And that convinced God that they practised bestiality to such an extent that they were even keen to copulate with his angels. This report was very effective in bringing down the fire and the brimstone upon them." Who knows whether that report was true. Who knows what was meant by *knowing?* Maybe the townsfolk simply wanted to *get to know* these mysterious beings. Nowadays, I suppose, we call it the spin that's put on an event. Now I lay my grandfather's book aside. I think of my own event, back on that train, in April. How the train quite suddenly came juddering to a halt. "The train up ahead has hit an object on the line." That was the announcement made, just as I opened my book to begin reading and dropped my spectacles at the same time. I glanced at the passengers sharing the carriage table. Goodness, I exclaimed. Do you think there's a body on the line? Who knows? said the jolly red-haired lady next to me.

He hit me on the back of the head with a night-stick. I went down like a nine-pin. 'Right, give me your cash.' As he knelt over me, I judged from his voice that he was white. Groggily I felt inside my pockets. His palm was pressing my chest, pinning me to the ground. I handed him whatever I found in my pockets: bank notes, car-keys – I was still only half-conscious. 'Can I keep my chips?' One minute, happy as Larry; the next, knocked to the ground. We drove to the hospital. I carried the Count inside and laid him on the bed... I took off the Count's jacket and tore away his shirt and undervest. I saw that he was wounded around the heart and that there was also a considerable quantity of blood on his clothes about it. When the doctor arrived, I asked if anything could be done, but he replied that it was too late, while my Uncle Paul might well have been that "third man", since he knew Philby at Westminster, and then at Trinity. Family weddings were presided over by Jack Putrall, the "red Vicar" of Thaxted. This Uncle, on my mother's side, wrote a book called *Nuer Law.* An anthropologist and officially a land-commissioner in the British Sudan, he was tall as a Nuer and identified with these tribesman. By far the worst part of being assaulted and robbed in the Old Kent Road was that I had handed the robber the keys to my Volkswagen van. Not that he knew which vehicle was mine, but later, the next day, that is, when I tried to drive away, a lump the size of an ostrich egg on the back of my head, there was no way into the van; to all intents it proved as sealed as the main gate of that compound in Constantinople. At the onset of the Greek War of Independence, as Ethnarch of the Orthodox Millet, Gregory V, Ecumenical Patriarch of Constantinople, was blamed by the Ottoman Sultan for his inability to suppress the Greek uprising, even though Gregory had actually condemned these revolutionary activities so as to protect the Greeks of Constantinople from reprisals. He was taken out of the Patriarchal Cathedral on Easter Sunday, directly after celebrating the solemn Easter Liturgy, and hung (in full Patriarchal vestments) for two days from the main gate of the Patriarchate compound by order of the Sultan; this was followed by a massacre of the Greek population of Constantinople. In his memory, the Saint Peter Gate, once the main gate of the Patriarchate compound, was welded shut in 1821 and has remained shut ever since. According to several accounts, after Gregory's death his body, along with those of other executed prelates, was turned over to the city's Jews, who dragged it through the streets and threw it into the sea. The accounts differ as to whether the Jews who did this were forced or had volunteered, but the tale spread like fire, and led to several bloody reprisals in southern Greece by the Greek rebels, who regarded the Jews as collaborators with the Turks. This in turn led to the Jews joining the Turks in attacks on Christians in some locations in northern Greece, which fuelled a new wave of anti-Jewish attacks in the south. Later, in 1917, surprise attacks on the Turks, attacks known as "line smashing" intensified. Raiding parties were led by Arab, French, and British officers. After packing camels with explosives and sometimes a Lewis machine gun or a Stokes mortar, they journeyed for a week or more into the desert. The men deployed exploder boxes as well as contact and electric mines. "Tulip mines" were popular because they twisted the Ottoman rails into tangled ribbons of steel. After one close call, British Lieutenant Stuart Newcombe returned to Egypt, his nerves shot. In hospital, his mind kept up its replay, as if he woke up and it was always the same day, the same time and place. "Right, Lads. Up and at 'em." Just as the shell landed in the midst of his patrol. "Right, Lads. Up and at 'em." As the nurses reported him muttering, over and over. Trapped in that moment forever, like the needle of the phonograph they carried with them that always stuck in that groove in the tango. Repetition and stasis are as much part of life as difference and inconsistency. Nevertheless, as Col. Pierce Joyce reported, "the noise of the dynamite going off was something grand and it is always satisfactory finding one is breaking things." Difference and inconsistency are as much part of life as repetition and stasis. In the west, it is easy to build up the illusion of continuity, security and an even tenor of existence, but then you have a seizure or a heart-attack. Life is a collage.

I was galloping under the oaks, my eyes raking the ground. Steeldust was going hell-for-leather. Then blank. And perhaps after that, or perhaps much later, days later even, a few frazzled half-memories:

oakleaves, worried looks, nothing clear to me now. But what I vividly recall is this. As if in a dream, I find myself on a horse. It is deepened dusk, practically dark. It is as if I have been woken up by the sound of the horse's hooves going clip-clop along a lonely country lane, hedges on each side. It is as if I have just been invented. Put together out of nothing, nothing that was there before this present, the present that I find myself in, sitting astride a horse, riding down a lane into the night. "Where am I?" I say, and a girl laughs, a girl riding on her own horse behind me. I recognise the voice. "Anthony, you've been saying that for the last half-hour."

They wanted to be sure I was taken off the train before I died. I am pretty sure of that. That's why they caused an obstacle to be placed on the line up ahead, so that the train ahead of us could be brought to a halt, slowing our own train down to a halt behind it. Therefore, our train is stationary, and I go into my convulsions, and a doctor is found and an ambulance is called, and I get placed on a stretcher and taken off our stationary express and slid into an ambulance and driven to the hospital where I have my second violent seizure, the one that is meant to kill me, far away from the train and its passengers, especially the two passengers who were sharing the table where I sat. To have had me die on the train would have been, to say the least, inconvenient. Inevitably, there would have been questions. I.D.s would have had to be established. There would probably have been interviews. As it transpired, the express had slid away from the embankment, and picked up speed, as the ambulance transported me to the hospital. By the time the second seizure occurred it would have regained its lightning velocity, practically arrived at Leeds, where I would have changed onto the train for Huddersfield, had I ever arrived. Leeds, where the two people who had shared my table – the slim rather languid girl with the long brown hair and the dark, slightly reluctant eyes and the more jovial, red-headed, buxom lady who had joined me in wondering what sort of obstacle had brought the train ahead to a halt – where these two would have passed through the barrier and vanished into the crowds milling through the streets. I'm wondering about all this as I sit in my London garden in my underpants, soaking up the sun. A blood-test taken after these seizures has shown that I am suffering from a massive lack of Vitamin D. I am sitting in the sunlit corner by the fig-tree. It is breakfast time. I am swallowing my pills with the aid of a glass of Badoit, munching my own version of a croque-monsieur, sipping my tea and allowing the sun to penetrate my flesh, sear my skin. I need the vitamin D. Only my eyes are shaded, by a generously-sized fig-leaf. There's a blaze of light from the sun above and behind this leaf.

There was a pinprick on my hand. There were wires coming out of me everywhere. My breasts were hurting as if I had just had all the periods of a whole year in one week. Oy vey! I was in diapers. How had I ended up here? And where was here anyway? I could see my Prada jeans, hung over a chair by the hospital bed. It was a hospital bed, that was for sure. I tried collecting my thoughts for once, not something I am in the habit of doing. LOL. I was Antonia Rosenbluth nee Lie. At least, I was yesterday. I used to be married to Sigurd Lie. Sigurd is a Norwegian anthropologist. We got divorced after our son died. We just couldn't cope. After we divorced, he went to study the Bedouin in Israel. I am a poetess. I know, I know. All my "me too" friends tell me to stop using the term "poetess". They tell me it's politically incorrect. But I maintain my preference for the word. The word exists for a purpose. It differentiates me from the males. And why not? If I was an actress, I would call myself an actress. I would consider it demeaning to call myself an actor. Poetess conjures up the image of wild Pre-Raphaelite locks. Locks like I've got. Fuck "Poet". What the fuck was I doing though, in diapers, feeling like shit in a hospital bed? I thought for a while, in a daze. There was this pinprick. It bothered me. This pinprick on my hand, a dark bruise surrounding it; nothing to do with the catheters or whatever they were, placed in the place inside where my forearm met my upper arm, monitoring my state, or carrying some fluid into me or out of me. A nurse came in and gave me some pills and glass of water. Hesitantly, I asked her where I was. She told me I was in Hinchinbrook Hospital, near Cambridge. I'd had a seizure on a train. I couldn't even remember the train. For some reason I could only remember Sigurd and Syria. Sigurd and I had visited the country more than a decade ago. We had gone in search of kelims. In those days we were both fascinated by the Middle East, and we travelled through Turkey and Iran, and finally, one year, we got as far as Syria, paying for our trip by selling our friends the kelims we had bargained for in every bazaar and souk we came across. A poet had given me a contact in Syria, a novelist no older than me. His name was Mamdouh Adwan. He took us to some wonderful places, crusader castles, agricultural settlements very like the kibbutzes Sigurd had visited years before in Israel, just on the other side of the Golan Heights. Mamdouh gave me this book he had written, *The Old Man and the Land*.

She joined the Israeli Defence Force as a soldier specialising in education, but later decided that she was meant for the field. Moving to Israel had transformed her. Literally. In Boston, what had she been? A pale, overweight girl of a somewhat phlegmatic humor. You could say she had emigrated to Israel: that would be to put a positive spin on her decision. Truer to say that she had fled Boston. Fled the

Rebecca she had been in Boston, brought up in an Orthodox family. Back in Boston, she just felt like a result. A sort of Yid commodity, produced by a mum as lethargic as she was herself. How cynical she had been, cynical and passive at the same time. Not that religious at all, until the last year or so, just going along with the rigmarole of it all. Taking it for granted, like it was taken for granted that if your mother was Jewish you were a Jew, whereas with only a Jewish dad, you could never be so sure. You could be the son or the daughter of some goyim whore. As if all mums were mice, obedient little mice, never compelled to stray, never willing to creep under the wrong side of the sheets. She had so wanted to change. To be a new Rebecca. What had the old Rebecca been but a victim? Having settled down on the kibbutz, she was made aware that she needed to shrug off all trappings of the Orthodoxy that had ultimately trapped her, back in the States. That heavy Orthodoxy that had switched off the lights automatically at the advent of the sabbath. It was just too heavy to lift, the weight of all those hidden things. Hidden family skeletons. Just as her own skeleton had been hidden deep within her pale, soft flesh, the flesh her grandad had first exploited. Passively enough, she had allowed him this transgressive exploitation. After all, she was hardly popular at school. For all her overweight mass, she was hardly noticed. She became background easily, simply part of the classroom or the playground, seen as a passive mass to most. At least her grandad noticed her, noticed how no one touched her, and then how easy it was for him to touch her, and just how easily she could be aroused. Perhaps he'd passed her on, after it became as clear as day his prostate had it in for him. And then there was Uncle Sol. It was just too heavy to lift. The depression following the exultation, the piercing, the being, the being the centre of his attention, and then, then being nothing, just his dirty secret. Better ignored. After her awareness was aroused on the kibbutz, she realised the answer was to enlist. And suddenly there was all this out-front condemnation. Perfectly straight. Directed at her. Rebecca, you're a fat, lazy cow. Now it's time to shape up. Shape up, do you hear? Yes, ma'am. Pick it up. Her kit was placed in front of her. All of it. She struggled. She simply couldn't get it onto her back. She muttered an apology, but the sergeant was having none of it. Pick it up, Rebecca. It was just too heavy to lift.

Running on lightning, we hurtle across the country. Stations flash past. I know what that is like. I can imagine myself standing on one of those platforms. Speed like an avatar. Gone, before seen. Slammed slap-bang into the future. But now I am aboard. Empowered. Well, not really. More like I'm riding on the power. Venomous voltage. I should get out my notebook. I should, I should. I've got it with me, together with the poems I will read tonight in Halifax. I have got them, haven't I? And my glasses? Yes. Yes, I've got everything. Why do I get so stressed? I guess it's because I don't have a car any more. I've got out of the habit of travelling. I've let myself become a big, pale lump of a man, sitting at my computer, starting out on a new poem, and then interrupting it to masturbate. They call it going to seed. Venomous voltage. Einstein comes to mind. Me stationary above this speeding energy. Lethal lines. While I am still, I'm stationary, at well over a hundred miles per hour. Fuck the bloody notebook, it's tucked away inside my inside pocket, and the large lady next to me will get my elbow in her bosom if I should try to get it out. Strange, really, how one changes. How one ages! I used to be what is called an intrepid traveller. My mother took me everywhere. It wasn't so much a matter of having a holiday as having an adventure. We visited my grandparents on the Jewish side, when I was three. They lived in New

York. Martin, my grandfather, was in charge of American funding for Israel. That would have been in '48. I got a certificate for crossing the Atlantic from the aircraft company. In those days you hopped from Shannon to Newfoundland, and then dipped down to New York. On the way back, by which time I was four, our plane developed a fault and we had to return to New York. No big deal. Blithely we went up the steps onto the next aircraft to cross the ocean. We went on skiing trips to Austria. We climbed mountains and got stuck on them and had to be rescued. We sailed from Venice to Greece. We stayed in a tent on Corfu. I remember the fireflies at night. Then we went on a mainland tour to Athens and to Delphi. We toured the Holy Land. Everywhere we went we had adventures. We rode ponies across the Hardanger Plateau, seeing no one for days, picking up discarded reindeer antlers, starting from one fjord and ending up at another. After I started travelling with my girlfriends or this wife or that, my mother went on travelling on her own. Her colleagues at the lab where she worked used to joke that wherever she went she started a war. She went to Hungary and started a revolution. I kept up the tradition she had inaugurated. I hitchhiked to Finland to visit a girlfriend. I hitchhiked to Ferrara. I recall that I once went to a reading by Andrew Motion, which he introduced by saying, "Recently I visited Amsterdam for the first time, and like you, the first place I visited was the house of Anne Frank." I raised my eyes and they rolled. That wasn't the first place I went, when I visited Amsterdam for the first time. Actually, I've never seen her house. I've seen the Prado, and the Hermitage, and the Kunst Kamera in Saint Petersburg, where Peter the Great gathered unto himself, all the freaks of nature he could find, and ordered by decree that all freaks, all two-headed cows, all giants, all weird and wonderful things conjured up in Russia should be sent to him, to become a part of the

Kunst Kamera collection. I visited Berlin, and Paris and New York and San Francisco. I went with my first wife to Iran. Later, we visited Syria, seeking out kelims.

You wake up each morning, don't you, memory intact? For "I saw one I knew, and stopped him, crying: "Stetson! You who were with me in the ships at Mylae! That corpse you planted last year in your garden, has it begun to sprout? Will it bloom this year?" Or am I you? For aren't your hands in the air? I am approaching the fence. Your soap is in my hand. I am approaching the chamber. Your spectacles are below me on the floor. I am bending down, to grope beneath the carriage table. And now my cap is on your head. You stand there on the dais, at the unveiling of the six-branched candle-stick with its seventh central stem.

If you are you, and not Razan. If I am me, and not Rebecca. If she is her, and not Adonai. If he is him, and not his grandfather. If you are Gregory V and not Lieutenant Stuart Newcombe. How can you tell? Who can you tell? Between sleeps or seizures, rapes or blows to the head. If your uncle is a sodomite, and not a cantor. If your father was a socialist, and not a Zionist. If you are a Jew, and not a Jew. If she is a Palestinian, and not a Palestinian. How can you tell? Who should you tell? Now that the Holy Land has become a Land of Smoke and Mirrors. Now that Sodom stinks of Milk and Honey? Sodom, whose people God has made blind.

I have her in my sights. She's barely ten years old. In another year she'll be eleven. I do like the backs of her knees. It's taken time to build her mother's trust in me. My brother doesn't count, her father that is. Too wrapped up in his Orthodox books, Talmudic references, stale items of Rabbinical esoterica for each new day of the year. He goes for that ancient look. Lots of locks. I don't believe he notices his family. Her mother runs the show at home. The spread cloth, the candle-sticks, the unleavened bread that's easy to get in Boston. Some say the British first offered us Uganda. Gateway to the Promised Land, they opined. Trying to get off the hook, wriggle out of the Mandate. And then there was that land by one of our great lakes, here in the States. That would have worked. Jews take to America like ducks to water. Whoever had ever been there before had already been genocided anyway – along with their buffalo probably – by the Founding Fathers. There is a corner of a foreign land that will be forever Jerusalem. You can find it in their Boston dining-room. Meanwhile, I'm feeling good. She's overweight, unpopular I guess. Makes it easier. Nevertheless that puppy-fat can't disguise a pale young sow just dying to be loved. Just as she should be. Just as she should. Keep it in the family. I bought her that cute little dress with its hem above the knee. That's our little secret. Her mum thinks she got it from another plumpish girl at school who'd gone ahead and developed. Pretty arse above the knees. Not so little either. Oh, God, I've got to use my shawl. Look, look at this, Rebecca. Isn't it as big as Baalbek? You can have it up you round the back. That way, no one will know. And there'll be no danger at all. And no one needs to know. No one needs to know that Eretz Israel has somehow morphed into Sodom.

Now my commanding officer wants me under surveillance at all times. I should never have done that shoot for the recruitment website. Someone has posted the pic on Facebook. The PR guy has been doing a pretty good job, saying that the image was generic, just a sniper image, not a sniper actually. Nevertheless, it's all over the media. Even if I didn't, it was me. Or I'm it, generically. I've been refused any leave. The whole squad has been taken off active service. Everyone blames me. Deborah won't talk to me, neither will Pinhas, neither will David, neither will Yehuda. The other David won't because he can't. He hung himself last year. I just feel I'm up against a ton of shit. Between a rock and a hard place. Like that massive step. That block I imagined a step. The first step in a staircase intending to go up, all the way to Paradise. Each step enormous. It would have been the very first wonder of the firmament. A staircase leading up to the heavenly garden. Mightily constructed, and designed to invite Jehovah to descend, to place his heavenly feet on earth. I said as much to Uncle Sol, as our guide went droning on in Baalbek. Uncle Sol said I was a fool. He only went to synagogue because he liked to sing, he said. We are a race, he would say, the Jewish race, that's what counts. We have no need of religion. That was why he had chosen to take us on this tour, as we were American citizens. Not to see the holy places, no, but to see what ancient Rome could do, in its own all-American way, or was it the Hellenic Greeks, out to outdo Rome? And to get to Petra, was his plan, my Uncle Sol, the rose-red city, its treasury carved out of its living rock. Between a rock. Between a rock. It was one hard place to get inside, just a narrow shaft of a canyon to get in or out. And, as Uncle Sol saw it, ours was a bargain trip: see the power of the ancient world, and get to see our relatives as well. And it was good, except for what he did. And that was before, before he started on Hava. I was awed by Baalbek. Heliopolis, that was its Classical name. The City of the Sun. In the Lebanon. I was more impressed by the quarry than the temples raised above it. That was where I saw that step. In the quarry there had been carved out a massive rectangular block of stone.

Since I increased the dosage I have been having these nightmares. First, there is a lion in my bedroom. I should never have agreed to this arrangement. There are complications. What these are is lost to me. I am too busy interviewing a big-time Russian criminal who is painting the interior of his maximum-security jail in colourful graffiti that extends down the corridors. When he gets out he will be welcomed by his supporters and wear some uniform with appropriate grandeur, at a distance, out of danger. Then there is some nasty business by a canal, and after that I am on a horse; we're jumping – fences, hedges, show-jumps? How can I tell? We're jumping whatever it is completely in the dark. One of us has been brutally murdered by the security forces of a heartless regime. Is it the Russians? My cousin turns up, hoping to stay at my place, but my place is no longer safe. We go to observe a pro-government demonstration. Even though it's pro-government, secret police are everywhere. It's not safe. My cousin says goodbye to a nurse. We have to get away right now. But I'm about to be apprehended, running up a hill. And now I am trying to get into a concentration camp, but the guards are hostile and turn me away. I am neither gay nor a Socialist. Neither a gypsy nor a Jew. I haven't got the right papers. I am trying to put together the parts of the flute I used to play when trying to play duets with my cousin Rafi in Tel Aviv. But the parts are mixed up with the parts of some quite other ancient instrument. Meanwhile my home in Holcombe Road has become the lion's lair. The lion has taken over my property. Most of the time his shadow is more apparent than his actuality. This shadow is massive, but most of the time it ignores me. Like the cat, the lion slips out of the bedroom window to get into the synagogue next door and have a pee, but it's easy for the cat to slip out of the window, not so easy for the lion who barely manages to squeeze through a window which only ever opens 45 degrees, though he just manages to do it by filling up the entire window with his massive haunches. I close and lock the window, and desperately I fight to draw the curtains which won't react to my tugging. They never do. They never fucking do. Then I am going to check all the windows in the house, eager to seal myself off from the garden, the synagogue and the lion. Then I am dressed in my white hospital coat and my red head-scarf. My hands are in the air. I am approaching the fence.

As the lazy sun slides towards the edge of the horizon, an old man, leaning on a rock on top of the hill overlooking the scorched plain, feels the earth still breathing out the heat and enveloping him in a lethargy which keeps him there with no desire to move or to walk home.

He looks around towards the plain at his feet and in his mind pictures the trees themselves suffering with him from the heat. They have their branches all curved down, as though wilting away. The land is so dry and thirsty that it looks as parched as his lips and throat.

Heat makes him angry and bad-tempered. He wishes he could be sick, or run away from himself. He wishes he had someone, anyone, to talk to; someone to whom to complain about the heat or indeed about anything that would help him shake away his lethargy and this sick feeling.

He pauses a moment, and lifts the back of his hand to his brow as though to wipe away the dust. Indeed, he reflects, he has no reason to be mad at himself, he has been working his land since dawn. But now that he's had to rest for the night, he feels he needs companionship. An acute feeling of loneliness grasps his heart and then seizes his whole body.

He did not feel this as much as he now feels it when Hassan Saleh left the village. True, he was angry when he woke up one morning and discovered that he had gone. But he had gotten used to this feeling of anger every time one or another of his neighbours went away and all signs of human life slowly drained out of these lands, day after day, since the end of the war.

Hadn't he woken every morning to learn that some people from the village had left for Damascus? Sometimes he saw them trudging along in the half-dark of dawn and felt an indefinable desire to weep. He wished he could run after them and beg them to stay. But he did nothing except quietly chew on his silent anger, to spit it out later, in the face of Hassan Saleh.

They used to sit alone in the twilight by the porch and review their memories. When they remembered one or the other of their friends Hassan Saleh invariably said, "I really miss him". He too missed the friend, and just as badly; but he would only show anger, bursting out with, "What a business had he to go, the accursed fool? Doesn't he appreciate Mansura anymore? You think he was afraid? Come on. It wasn't fear. What is there to be afraid of? The Jews? Here we are since the end of the war, both alive and well. Nothing is going to befall us, but by the will of God."

Even when that Israeli officer came up to the village with some soldiers and ordered everybody to leave, threatening to shoot any person staying within two hours, he'd not felt scared but went home quietly – as though the threat was not intended for him.

The soldiers came back. Some of the people had been scared away, but most of the villagers had stayed on in their homes. The soldiers rounded them up in the village square, they chose three young men, tied their hands behind their backs, lined them along a wall and shot them. They warned the awe-struck, unbelieving onlookers that the same fate awaited those who chose to stay on.

When the soldiers had gone, the old man helped to give the three victims a decently religious burial, and then walked slowly home, sad and full of anger. But he was neither afraid nor willing to quit.

Daily now, an exodus of people from other villages passed by. They told stories of carnage, of explosions, and the annihilation of whole villages. Stories which made the hackles rise or the hair stand on end. The old man did not see why he should doubt the truth of their stories. He had, all through his life, heard of the atrocities these invaders committed everywhere, but he never imagined that one day they would pull Mansura down and that he would be killed.

The others got away by night. For nine months this human haemorrhage went on. Hassan Saleh remained a month longer, as a last drop may linger a moment after the rest of the blood has drained, but even this must fall at last. "Go to the devil, then. You would have stayed on longer if there were any good in you. Your presence or your absence makes no difference to me. Did you think I would have held you back for my own sake? Do whatever you like! If only if I had someone to speak to now, about your running away!"

And so he wished Hassan were still there, sitting by the porch. It's good to exchange ideas in the twilight... We would have talked, or maybe had an argument. Hadn't we perfected the art of arguing with one another? The old man remembered their last quarrel:

What are these?

They're seeds, of course.

Seeds?

Naturally. Don't you know what seeds are?

What do you need seeds for?

Good God, here is Hassan Saleh, asking me what I need them for!

You can't mean you are going to sow your seeds! Man, I just don't get you anymore!

Do I look like I'm joking?

Now let me get this straight. Is there something wrong with your mind?

God of the prophet! What a dumb brute you are, Hassan. Do you want me to split your head with this?

He gestured with his axe.

Is it that you're trying to split my head?

You old, demented fool, use your head. Does any sensible man sow in such times as these?

Does one not eat in such times?

I see, you reckon on staying.

And why not?

The seeds, they're for sowing this Autumn?

Of course, we have to think of tomorrow.

If you'd ever properly thought of tomorrow you'd have long since gone away.

Back to the same old tune? Why don't you go then, if you're so logical?

Don't you see how death surrounds us now?

I told you before. I'm not in the mood to die!

God decides these matters, Idriss.

I'll decide. I'm not going to die!

God forgive us, Idriss, don't, don't be blasphemous!

I mean when God decides to take my life, that's up to him, but russin then I'll not allow myself to die of hunger, I'll have a better ending, that I shall.

You're going to die with a bullet up your butt!

And you will die of death, Hassan; of your constant worry about death. Look, when they come to kill you, they'll find nothing left.

Don't you get it, you crazy fool? They can shoot you any time, if they haven't done it yet it's because you're just an old demented harmless sort of nut.

Shut up, Hassan! That's what you are.

I liked my making him angry, I liked his limited understanding. Our quarrels lasted but a moment. Now I wish he were here so that I could provoke him into shouting out again.

But he knew Hassan Saleh could not ever again be there, he knew everyone had gone and he was left, this lone tree, upright on the scorched plain.

He'd always doubted that Hassan would stay long after the others had gone. Still, he had the merit, at least, of being the last one to go. He was always very much in fear, scared by any rumour, eager to believe whatever he heard. He even credited what that Israeli soldier had said, when he told them that this land was theirs, and that they had come to recover it.

Did you hear them, Idriss, they say the land is theirs?

Idriss laughed. He laughed as if it were a good joke. Then he explained what liars these people were.

This land belongs to Hassan Saleh and Idriss and Khaled and Hilal, none of whom seem to me to be Israeli. I don't think there was in any man's living memory a time when the land belonged to people other than this village's people. And is there a Jew among them? No, not one. Let alone an Israeli Jew.

Ah, but they say it is Israeli, theirs since thousands of years.

Idriss laughed again and said:

Yes, maybe, if Mohamed were Jewish, and Antara, and Abu Zeid Hilali and if all the Arab heroes you hear about were Jewish. Come on, Hassan. How can you believe such trash?

The poor fool, forever scared! What is he scared of at his age? It seems that the older one gets the more one clutches onto life. And he was afraid, not only for himself, but also for those who had run away to other parts of Syria.

Do you think they are safe?

Of course they are, why are you so worried?

I don't know, I just keep on worrying!

Are you worried about me as well? Don't forget I am two years older than you, so you can forget about me.

You fool, even a kid's got far more sense than you. Where have you been?

What woke you up at this hour?

I heard some shooting... so I came to see if you were safe, I was worried not to find you at home.

Worried about me, Hassan, or about yourself?

Where were you?

I went out to take a look. They're having shooting exercises.

To take a look? You're mad!

Why not take a look? To tell the truth, I go there every day, to take a look.

At the Jews?

No, I look at the lights of Damascus.

And Idriss turned and looked towards Damascus. But a light mist had dimmed the distant lights and he saw nothing but the darkness of the deep night. Yet he knew the flickering lights would soon reappear. And so he waited.

Our jeep goes hell-for-leather across the terrain. I'm feeling a bit queasy. It was the start of my period yesterday. Joseph is telling me how, while I was on leave for the day, the week before, our squad had been sent to ensure the safety of a team of settlers. They were intent on taking down a grove, so their truck was loaded with chain-saws. By the end of the day, they had sliced through a couple of hundred trees. The shits were out in force of course, doing their wailing and holding their hands over their ears. Some of the olives had been there for over two hundred years. As Joseph sees it, the olive groves represent some sort of continuity to the shits. And this conflicts with the continuity of the promise. That is, the promise to us. Because we have suffered enough. He has made His decision. We shall not be the victims any longer. Besides, with modern methods of irrigation we don't really need all these gnarled old Mediterraneans. Joseph is the thinker in our squad. He reckons we need to fertilise, get rid of all the stones that prop the olive roots up as these sad old trees begin to lean. Bring in newly imported loam and plant some European crop. We have to break their continuity, he says. What's ours is ours, just as the promise grants it us. But that means imposing our identity. Their land has to be changed. Otherwise, to the shits, well, it sort of remains their land. I'm feeling bloody below. Need to change my tampon. But we're moving fast. Loam from Poland, Joseph suggests. We are driving down towards Beersheba. Five k south there's unrest. So we've been sent to pacify. Scattered around the Negev are some villages we've scheduled for demolishment. Joseph says the villages are just a contradiction in terms. Why should the fucking Bedouin have villages? They're supposed to live in fucking tents. Goat-hide tents, like in the old brown photos. Their whole ethos has been moving on, following the grazing, or moving to fresh water-holes, so why the fucking villages? We take a right down a track made by previous tires. We on the alert because of the dunes. That's why we've been sent to protect the demolition crews. These dunes enable the shits to appear out of nowhere. These Bedouin shits should stick to their own fucking ethos. So, we are moving them on? That's what they are meant to do. Move on, on their fucking camels. Camel after camel after camel.

Our shooting platform's designed by FAB Defense. It's really neat. You set it up on its tripod. Fine tune the adjustment. Camel after camel after camel. Can I have this one? Get down on your tummy, check your sights. And you just know the guys are checking you out, checking out your butt, that is, spread-eagled, in your camouflage fatigues. You looked good today, Pinhas says. He turns me on. His name. Sounds like penis. Camel after camel went down the front of my zip-up jacket. It wasn't that I was stealing them exactly. I just added another, and then another. I think the shop-keeper in the bazaar thought I was simply swapping one for another. They were all broken anyway, not the camels themselves, the chains that held them together in sets of three. I became pregnant with camels. He was intent on selling this lizard skin bag to my mother. He thought I was choosing another *instead* of the one I had chosen before. It had a lizard's face on the clasp of its flap. Can I have this one? Of course, of course. Can I have this one? Can I have this one?

Our commanding officer gets us all to watch *Day of the Jackal.* He has it screened as part of our training. He says it shows how methodical you have to be. A sniper's blood is cold, he says. It has to be. Ensure that your platform's secure. Check the spirit level. Choose your target. Fix on it. That's just what I do. I never fire on first sight. First, I identify. Then I follow. Cool and smooth. Then I calculate where exactly my target has to be for me to get my best shot. It has to be said that the shits can be quite accurate as well. You really need to rethink that David and Goliath stuff. Think it through again.

That thug of a Philistine might have been all muscle. But he was up against superior technology. That's the way it is here, except that the technology has moved on. But still, when we drove back up from the Dead Sea, it was great when we stopped by the Bedouin to take snaps of their tents, and great that the dark-eyed shepherd boy was happy for me to get his sling in exchange for a couple of shekels. Not that I ever got to work out how to use it. Had I stayed among them, travelled with them through the mountains of Moab, he would have shown me just how to use it. But the coach needed to move on, and besides, I was only ten. We had touched down in Jordan the day before, flying over Syria from the Lebanon. And that flight is not something I'll ever find hard to remember. The River Jordan writhed below us, writhed like a holy snake.

"The Minister dances. Why does he dance?"
A caption to a cartoon. Great-uncle Pinchas Rosen
Twirling a finger above his head in Beersheba.
Dancing, yes, I remember him, dancing
There in the dust of that dirt-floored square.
And he was nearly seventy then, hopping
And kicking and stamping among
The local Bedouin, till gaiety dissolved their stare

And they smiled at him – *and* at the ten-year old me –
As they looked on or danced with him
As he danced, like the statesman he was,
Danced as a statesman there, to show solidarity.
And that was back when one could dream
Of wholeness in that forward-looking
Land of refuge from the camps – with orange
Groves and falafel to adore.

But why does he dance, asked the press,
Just at a time when several Kibbutzim
Had come under fire. Why? But this is the time for it,
He would say, Uncle Felix, as he was to me.
He told me once that cultural exchanges
Were generally more likely to materialise
When matters had chilled between nations.
"So, if you want your enterprise

Sent here to perform for us, cause an international
Ruckus, nice little mess that sours
The relationship between your government and ours!"
Today I bear a big bald pate like his one.
Minister of Justice in the days of Golda Meir,
He felt obliged to resign when Ben Gurion
Refused to let him prosecute a friend of his
For past collaboration with the Axis.

"History, old history, my boy." Yes, but why
Did they dance, the five dancing Israelis?
Why did they dance in the wake of the towers
Elsewhere in Manhattan? People saw them:
Dancing in the shadow of catastrophe,
Dancing in its aftermath around a plain white van.
It seems important that they should have been
Seen dancing, then arrested, then sent home.

"By way of deception" – was there another white van?

I called this poem *Dancing Israelis,* and I captioned it with the motto of Mossad. "By way of Deception, thou shalt do War." I got the lines about Ben Gurion from some family member, and now I wonder what this could possibly be referring to. At the time I heard the tale, I assumed it to be some business partnership Ben Gurion was involved in. Now I wonder if it didn't refer to the Nazi Otto Skorzeny, who had agreed to assassinate a German scientist called Krug for Mossad. This was an operation Ben Gurion may have endorsed. Krug, the scientist, was helping Egypt develop missiles. Skorzeny, a notorious commando decorated by Hitler, carried out the assassination as planned, after Krug was induced to contact Skorzeny in the hope that the great hero – then living in Spain – could create a strategy to keep the scientists safe. The two men met in Munich. They were driving North out of the city in Krug's white Mercedes, and Skorzeny said that as a first step he had arranged for three bodyguards. He said they were in a car directly behind and would accompany them to a safe place in a forest for a chat. That was the end of Krug. Skorzeny's reward was to be taken off Simon Wiesenthal's list. It is this that my Uncle Felix, as Minister of Justice, may well have objected to, given his well-known regard for probity. I wrote the poem about a year ago, when I was seventy-two. Back when the Minister danced, I was proud to be in Israel. Proud to stand by my Uncle's side, not in my zip-up jacket but in my school uniform, as the six-branched Menorah was unveiled. I think it must have been the Knesset Menorah in Jerusalem. This is a bronze candle-stick. With six branches around its single central stem, it's known as a seven lamp. It's 4.30 meters high and 3.5 meters wide. This one weighs four tons. It is located at the edge of the Rose Garden, opposite the Knesset. It was designed by Benno Elkan, a Jewish sculptor who escaped from his native Germany to Britain. It was presented to the Knesset as a gift from the Parliament of the United Kingdom on April 15, 1956 in honour of the eighth anniversary of Israeli independence. That makes me ten years old at the time. It was inaugurated on 15th April. Five days before my eleventh birthday. It does explain why my Uncle, that is, my Great Uncle, who was leader of the progressive party, took me by the hand and led me onto the platform among the Ben Gurions and the Golda Meirs, to witness this unveiling, since I was an honest-to-god, authentic British schoolboy. I wonder now whether it was he who paid for our flight – just so that I could become a part of the ceremony. This Knesset Menorah was modelled after the golden candelabrum that had stood in the Temple in Jerusalem. A series of bronze reliefs on it depict the struggles to survive of the Jewish people: formative events, images and concepts from the Hebrew Bible and from the Zionist version of Jewish history, so engravings on the six branches of the Menorah portray episodes since the Jewish exile from Eretz Israel, as my grandfather loves to call it in his book *Go Forth and Serve*. Those on the central stem portray the fate of the Jews from the return to the land to the establishment of the State. It has been described as a visual "textbook" of Jewish history. Great Uncle Felix was a believer in proportional representation. His children were all liberals. However, my mother was Labour. As a Ministry vet, she had spent the war bringing peace to the cows maimed in the Essex fields, when German planes discarded their stick-bombs before heading back across the Channel. When not bringing peace to the cows, she was helping to rehouse blitzed families in East London or refugees. She always insisted that proportional representation would bring about Israel's downfall. As a socialist, she had mixed feelings about Zionism, and that is perhaps why she decided we should see "both sides" and arranged for us to join a tour that took in the Lebanon, and Baalbek, and the Palestinian refugee camps, and the old city of

Jerusalem, which was then still part of the Kingdom of Jordan. We just flew over Syria.

Judah is a lion's whelp. From the prey, my son, you are gone up: he stooped down, he crouchéd as a lion, and, as a lioness, who shall rouse him up? Who indeed would wake a fucking lioness, the female fiercer than her mate? In Boston, everyone was fat. Fat, clumsy citizens of a rank hotchpotch of states. Stuffed with fast food, immobilized by their cancer-causing screens. Here, we are lean and fit. I can move swift as a snake under the wires. Back in America, I was abused. Just another fat, immobile teen. You could turn me on just be touching me. My grandad knew how to do it. I was a daughter of Lot. I was a fat, immobile slut. Deborah nodded. Rebecca reached for a cigarette. That's why I like the name Yehuda. Here I'm like a lion's daughter. Fuck it, fuck that "Me too" shit. Me, I turn my back on being any sort of a victim. Crawling, insect life. Me, I take my prey and carry it up, into the mountains. Way up there, in the crags, that is where I make my lair. Victimhood's for sluts, I say. She took a slug from the flask. The moon above them seemed to swell. Israel is strong. A strong place that makes her daughters stronger than any fucking uncles. Israel's made me a man. Made me a fucking killer. Don't you wake me up, you dirty-minded, overweight old git. Waking up a lioness. Shit, you risk your life. The moon had a cloud thrown over it. In the dark, there was just the reek of their cigarettes. The taste of whiskey in their throats. Perhaps it's the camps that have made us like we are now, Deborah said. Teeming insect life, muttered Rebecca. Yes, I guess it's the camps. The way they just lay down, took it lying down, that is. Stripped down to your skin, given what looked like a bar of soap, herded off down some corridor into the showers. Never again. Never, Deborah echoed her friend. The moon reappeared, emphasising the dark ridge of the barracks roof behind them. That's what I've always felt about the shits. I saw their camps. Dirty fucking acres of them, fences keeping us from them. They took it lying down. I saw it when my Uncle Sol took us on this tour when I was ten. We visited the Lebanon. I had my U.S. passport. On the way back from Baalbek, we noticed them, cooped up behind the fences. There we were in our nice, luxury coaches, there was this trim, dry verge of grass and there they were for us to cruise past, fucking dirty shits. Frankly, I felt nothing but contempt. She took another slug. Teeming insect life, said Uncle Sol. I think of teeming insect life whenever someone mentions concentration camps.

Many modern poisons leave no trace. Smear the stuff on a door-knob. No need even to administer it by making a prick in the skin. She could have just smeared my Ribena. Simple enough, with a handker-chief, just as I leant over for a doze against the carriage window. Still, it's all peculiar. One moment I'm heading off into a doze, and then, the next moment, or maybe it's still part of that same moment, I'm being hauled out of my seat, stretched out on a stretcher. Yes, ok, it's all very well. That is how it appears to me now. That is what I recall. But then, before we were into the hospital, I'd conked out again. Who was I in that interval of lying horizontal? Double windows at the back of the ambulance. Tree-tops, and what felt like country lanes. Finally I came to again, clad in nappies. Soaked jeans caught the corner of my eye, hanging, as they were, over the back of a chair. Where was I? Well, more urgently, I wondered who I was. For that is all that comes back to me. And what is weird is that all of it comes back to me as being of a piece. As if I were still Anthony. But what I want to know is, was I Anthony? Isn't memory itself a sort of fiction? Was I Anthony, before? Before I found myself in this hospital, which turned out to be somewhere near Cambridge? I found myself, I say. I came to my senses. But how can I be sure I found myself? How can I be sure that the senses I came to were those of whoever I was before the fit? Clearly I'd been drugged up to the tens. Astonished to be suffering the indignity of waking up in nappies. Who had put the nappies on me? Ever since, I have wondered about this. Wondered about identity. How we just take it for granted. Just as I took it for granted that I was a boy with a grey windcheater jacket with an elasticated waist, a jacket that zipped up at the front. How we take for granted our deictic centre. I being here, in the here and now, while you are there, and he or she is there. We take "now" for granted. We take "here" for granted. We take the past for granted, and…we even take the future for granted. And although I happen to be recalling it now, because the now is all I can possibly know, I grant myself some continuity by bringing up some memory to prove it. How smart everything was in the Lebanon. Ultra-modern hotel. Large luxurious coaches. The hotel manager telling my mother that as far as he was concerned, he saw no reason why the Lebanon should not get on in a civilized way with Israel, their neighbour. For hoteliers, there were opportunities for business partnerships. Neatly-cropped palms accompanied the esplanade on the seafront. From my point of view, it was all a bit dull. Beirut, I mean. We only stayed a night or two. The aim was to visit Baalbek. The coach took us there, the next day, in a party of Americans led by a Methodist preacher. I think it was there that a camel bent over a gaunt old American called Mrs Watson and calmly began to eat her hat. And the thing was, Mrs Watson looked very much like a camel herself. Baalbek was immense. Six enormous columns standing alone, holding up a section of the entablature above. Jupiter's temple. Set there to impress. Don't mess with the Roman Empire. Or was it the Greeks, endeavouring to out-impress those up-and-coming Romans? Was it built by the civilisation that enabled Noah to build his Ark? Or was it the site of the Tower of Babel? No, I am sure that's the stadium that is going up now, at White Hart Lane, easily seen from my bedroom in Tottenham Hale. The platform at the temple's base is called the stylobate. This was kept simple in Baalbek, since it had one simple job to do: keep the whole edifice standing. Standing on mighty stylobate blocks. And now, well, there are these six columns. That is all that's left, but perhaps, that is all that ever got built; the project never completed. Look on my works, ye mighty, and despair. This was the city known as Heliopolis. There are temples to Venus and to Mercury as well as to Jupiter, and there is one dedicated to Bacchus. At ten years of age, I knew all the stories, could tell you all the myths. I felt like an ant as I threaded my way between the 20-metre-high columns. Mum suggested that was their intention, to make you feel like an ant. "Any description of what an ant is doing must include what its environment is doing." Since my seizures I've been reading quite a bit of Alan Watts. If the student takes the ant's environment into account, then "the thing or entity he is studying and describing has changed. It started out to be the individual ant, but it very quickly becomes the whole field of activities in which the ant is found." So therefore, my identity is the whole field of activities in which I am found, or anyone else. Back then, it was the Lebanon, and a small boy and his mum on a Methodist tour that would take in the supposed tomb of Christ; a cell-like cube, hollowed out of precipitous rock below Golgotha. Here our Methodist guide would preach for hours, while it rained quite miserably outside. Baalbek was far better, to my mind. More a place that conjured up mythology. Heading back to Beirut though, there were other sights. Coming back from Baalbek, our coach drove past the camps.

Maybe I was her yesterday. Maybe she was me. Back in Boston, my brother used to have seizures. His eyes would go all glazed. Sometimes he would collapse. Sometimes he would remain conscious, or so it seemed, but then he would make these strange remarks. No, Uncle Sol. I don't want to do it. Please. Don't put me into the freezer. Things that didn't make sense. You asked him about what he'd said later, and he couldn't remember having said anything. He told me once that when he came round, he could never be sure that he had come round. Or that he had been himself before he'd had the seizure. I could have been you before, he told me once, or dad or mum. I don't really trust who I am that I appear to have come round as. Do you get what I mean? I mean I could have been Cassius Clay, or Mohamed Ali, or whatever he calls himself nowadays. How do I know? I've gone and lost track of myself. I told him I was perfectly sure he was David, just as he had always been. The David I grew up with and who had grown up with me. He looked at me in disbelief, or something that resembled disbelief. After dad died, we saw quite a bit of our uncles. Uncle Sol in particular, and Aunt Mitzie. Uncle Sol would tell me that if David had a seizure I was to stick a spoon in his mouth, to stop him swallowing his tongue. Uncle Sol supplied stuff for the army, we were told. He was also our cantor. He had a big, fruity sort of voice. Uncle Sol just liked to sing, he told me, that was it, he just got into the singing. Unlike Uncle Benjie. He was ultra in his views, just as our dad had been, a pillar of the synagogue and all that. I thought he was creepy. Most of our uncles were, one way or another. And Uncle Sol did pretty well out of supplying the military with gear. He would take mum and me and Hava and David on cruises. Usually Aunt Mitzie stayed at home, to run things, as he said; taking care of their place and our own. One year, we set out on a tour, a tour of the holy land.

He gave her all the love that still filled his heart; the love he used to lavish on his wife and children. Long hours were spent in talking to her or in quietly looking at her, as though listening to her conversation.

You are lonely as well, he used to say, but no matter, don't be afraid. Then he would stretch out his hand to stroke her neck and scratch her brow. Her calf had died during the war – a year after his wife passed away. The children, and all their relatives and their neighbours had gone. Now he was left alone with only his cow for company.

And though he was deeply fond of her and enjoyed talking to her, he often shied away from looking into her face for fear he would catch some sign of reproach.

Her calf had died in the war, so to make her go on giving her milk, Idriss had had the calf stuffed and placed in the barn. He dared not look into her eyes when he milked her, for he sensed he was stealing by taking advantage of her feelings. This sensation of guilt somehow spoiled their friendship.

His satisfaction in serving her was equal to his satisfaction in working the land. He had worked late today and the cow had eaten and drank well. Why should he be worried?

Why did those two soldiers look so strangely at her today?

Did the thought of taking you cross their mind? God forbid it! Anything but you! Now I have no one left but you, my dear. Imagine how I would be, now all the children and the neighbours have gone… Utterly alone.

He did not want to pull her by the rope that tethered her, but put his arm around her neck and coaxed her along.

He feels hungry when he comes close to the house. It's been his wont to feel hunger every time he approaches the house or even sees it from afar. But today the hunger is mixed with that sense of loss and a desire to weep, yet his feet still cover the ground with determination, as he approaches the door.

He remembers other summers, and his first days of marriage when he used to come back from the hunt with a score of birds, or maybe a hare, if he had been lucky. He would throw the birds over the wall before entering the courtyard. All too often, his wife would warn him to stop such nonsense. She wasn't always there in the yard, and the cat, or a stray dog might snap up the birds and make a run for it. But Idriss knew she was there, every time he came back, waiting for him to chuck them over the wall. She had got used to his habits fairly quickly. He liked to busy himself around the house when he was not in the fields; but when he came back from his hunting, he always went off to the village shop to chat with other villagers. For the best part of an hour, he'd exchange news with Abou Hani the shopkeeper or with the soldiers on leave at the village.

When he came back home, he was invariably greeted at a distance by the smell of cooking. His wife was an excellent cook as well as an excellent housekeeper. Everyone in the house liked her, including the cow, who used to follow her silently around the courtyard or to the field, and stood still and confident, whenever she was milked.

Again, he strokes the cow's neck, and when they reach the house, he does not lead her directly into the barn, but ties her to the door, as though he wanted her to share with him the beauty of the twilight.

It was pretty clear they wanted to steal the cow. Did they know she was alone? Maybe one of them had killed her calf. Could he not have been the pilot of the plane that had swooped down, spitting lead and fire? Several people had needed to be buried that day. Many animals had died as well. And that night, all through the night, the cow would not stop calling her calf, keeping Idriss awake and keeping his anger on the boil. Maybe they wanted to take her now. She was a very fat cow. A cow that might tempt anyone. If they did not want to take her, why were they surprised to see him there? Why did they laugh so strangely?

Again, Idriss feels the deep anger that had seized him in the morning, when he'd observed how they'd looked at him and burst out laughing. He was sure they were laughing at him.

What is so funny about me to make them guffaw so unashamedly? Is it my old age? How is a man supposed to look after turning sixty? Don't they have ageing parents? Cursed be their parents and the parents of their parents! If they knew my real age they wouldn't laugh. A man at this age should be tilted over, bent, coughing incessantly.

What was there to make them laugh? Was it his appearance? There was no question about it: his appearance called for respect. Wherever he went, he walked with conviction. There had not been a villager who didn't stand up when he greeted him. They all came to him for advice and asked him to solve their problems, even though at times his relatives or sons happened to be involved in their dispute.

Why, then, did they laugh at him? Was it because they intended to fool him by stealing his cow some day? True he had turned to her and said, my dear, I shall protect you with the pupils of my eyes. Was this actually funny enough to make them laugh so long at him?

How impolite, to scoff at his words! He's sure they understood very little though of what he'd said. The tallest one could pronounce a few Arabic words, while the other looked at him with a stupid smile on his face and spoke an ugly language; a language which the old man could not understand.

Even suppose they understood Arabic perfectly, what did I say to make them laugh? I always weigh my words, before I say a thing.

Idriss had lifted his eyes and seen them coming towards him. He had put aside all memory of the war and waited for them to approach him without the least anxiety. At first he had even imagined that they were Syrian soldiers, those he used to meet now and then, either at Abou Hani's or in the narrow streets of the village or at the fountain. Soldiers had always been a part of daily life in the village. One of them had married a girl there, another had tried to court one . . . Soldiers making passes at girls on their way to the fountain, or seeking out a woman to beat the dirt out of their clothes. Some of the villagers praised the soldiers, who protected the border. Others hated them because they were capable of stealing the crop or digging some trench or road through a field, ruining the soil.

He expected these two to pass by without speaking to him. This sense lasted no more than a fraction of a second. After that he remembered. This was war. There was no ignoring the defeat. He realised they were enemy soldiers. He looked at them inquiringly and saw in their faces an astonishment which angered him. It was infuriating, his being unable to understand what was going on in their heads.

The short blond young fellow saw him first. He pointed him out to his buddy as they came near with broad smiles on their faces.

Hello, said the tall one in broken Arabic, showing off his learning to his pal.

Good morning, answered the old man dryly, showing no interest at all.

What is this? asked the tall guy.

The old man found the question exceptionally stupid, but he did sense that it was asked in earnest and did not hide any threat to him or mockery. Nonetheless, he chose now not to answer, just resumed his work, calmly ignoring their presence.

He had been a little scared when he saw them approaching. Never in his life had he seen Israeli soldiers, well, not until the war came, when he discovered that they were often handsome blond young men. He used to be of the opinion that they could utter nothing but threats and stir in one no feeling besides fear and loathing. But when they asked that stupid question, Idriss felt contempt. He felt himself to be in a superior position, here on his own land. Only the most stupid of men could fail to notice that he was digging a ditch.

I say! shouted the blond, short one. The old man looked at him inquiringly. The tall one gestured with his hand towards the ditch and asked:

Water?

The old man nodded his confirmation.

What for, the water?

By all the prophets, his head almost split! How could one ask such question? Why dig a ditch? Why does one dig a ditch? Doesn't this baboon know the usefulness of water to the earth? Once more the old man held onto his silence.

The tall one went on in his broken Arabic.

You alone?

The old man lifted his head angrily:

How do you know?

I know.

The soldier smiled. The old man said nothing. The soldier went on:

You alone now. Why? Why tire yourself digging?

Why? Idriss could spend an hour in answering that. But he already sensed that they would never get it. And so, he simply replied:

For water.

Yes. But why water?

Now it seemed that the tall one thought him stupid. Idriss spelt it out.

To water the fields.

But you alone, not so?

I am.

The short one turned seriously towards his companion. They talked in that incomprehensible language which made him so irritated. The tall one turned to him.

Where the spring ?

The old man raised his hand towards the nearby spring. The short one went scuttling in that direction with two canteens. While these were filled, the tall one squatted beside the old man and renewed the conversation.

Why tire yourself digging if you alone?

The old man quietly scrutinized the soldier's face. He observed that it was very thin and in bad need of a shave. His anger had mounted so high, he thought it best to play deaf.

I not understand why you work.

And they pretend that it's their land, their soil. If only Hassan Saleh could hear this, with his own ears! Of course you don't. You would understand it though, had you some land of your own to work on.

Idriss turned to the soldier and decided to explain, using his hands to ensure that the brute would comprehend.

There was war. . . many bombs came down. . . you understand?

The young man shook his head, though listening intently.

The old man went on, as though explaining to a child.

Many women and children died besides our men. Animals died as well, you understand? This cow lost her little one. In the war. The calf was only two months old. You understand?

Yes, I understand.

The war ended. Soldiers like you came and ordered us to go. They shot three young men who refused to go. You understand?

Yes but. . .

Everyone was scared away, you understand?

I understand, I understand. You are alone, so what use is your work?

A ditch here is useful. The village people wanted to start digging it. Were it not for the war it would already have been dug.

But now everybody go… What use?

They'll need to water the land when they come back.

Come back?

Of course! They are a little late, of course, but it doesn't matter much, they will be back here today or tomorrow.

Now the tall soldier laughed aloud. The old man was maddened by this laugh which sounded full of irony. The short young man squatting beside him laughed so hard, he lost his balance. Not that he understood a word. But what had Idriss said to make them laugh so merrily? He looked at them hard, wondering whether they were in full possession of their faculties. Between one peal of laughter and another, the taller fellow called to his companion:

Hey, Andre!

He made signs with his hands while talking and laughing at the same time. Then they both started laughing again.

The old man looked at them haughtily until at last they stopped.

The tall one came closer as he dusted the bottom of his pants. He said, go on digging, have no fear. We'll be over there.

He gestured to the ridge.

They walked away still laughing loudly. As they passed the cow, he thought he saw them look at her. He stopped digging:

Let them but touch her and I will teach them to laugh. This young lad is too full of himself. Their guns are no match for my shovel.

Idriss gripped the handle with both hands.

Later that day, stretched on the porch at dusk, he thought he felt their eyes observing him from afar…still convulsed with laughter.

The shame of the matter is that they think I have need of their protection.

He recalls the words of the tall one: Go on digging. Have no fear.

Fear? Fear of what? And who is to reassure me if I do feel fear? This young baboon? I have experienced fear in my life, fear they've never dreamed of.

He'd had a fear of policemen, but even with them, his fear had driven him to face them, while others slid away. He had once been very much afraid – once, while crossing a torrent. He had feared that the wild waters would pull him down with the current. He'd been afraid, but still he had crossed there, while fear prevented all his friends from crossing. Like all people in the village, the war had scared him even more. He'd been afraid that he might be hit by a stray bullet or consumed by napalm. He'd been afraid his house would he bombed or his crops burnt. When the village people met, their individual fears merged into one collective shock. Some suggested that they move to Damascus, but Idriss opposed the suggestion as did some other villagers and so he'd stayed on, along with his fears.

When one or the other of them had tried to justify moving to Damascus, by saying, they killed him and they killed them and they'll certainly kill us, or someone else came up with, war is blind, you shouldn't put yourself at risk, find a place to set your mind at rest, Idriss had not been able to accept these views. True, he could not counter them with any great conviction of his own. In reality, he found that he had no wish to get involved in any discussion whatsoever, and so he would invariably leave the meeting in anger. This haemorrhage of villagers went on and on until it ended at last, with the departure of Hassan Saleh.

Even worse was when people fleeing from neighbouring villages passed through his village in a sad stampede. Their fear caused ripples all round as they spoke of whole villages being blasted, of indiscriminate killing, of attacks on women and children. Nobody mentioned the land itself. Go, they cried, and he would cry, Where to? Watching them as they left, carrying as much as they could of their belongings.

Where are you to go?

It's going to be our turn next.

Yes, but the land?

What can we do about that? God must look after it. We have to think first of our women and our kids.

But you don't have to be scared away. Your life is not just yours. Who is going to rebuild Banias, Kafr Hareb and Ain Ziwan? And what about Mansura? You've got to be there – some of us have to – so we can help each other.

Not no one had the time to listen. How stupid it was of everyone to see but one aspect. Had they had my age and experience they would have known what life really is. They should have been around in the forties, when we had the great snow. All the evergreens seared, right down to their roots. But the roots remained. Hidden beneath the earth, they withstood it all. When spring returned, the land was again coated with green, as before. They are nothing but children, he thought, recollecting how he used to tease them. He smiled as he remembered how Abou Ali used to sweat, unable to return his cutting words. I will remind him of the words he used to repeat so often, when he gets back: I tell you if I have to die in this war, I will welcome death. But where is he now, Abou Ali? Has he gone to Damascus? Is it there he'll welcome death?

The old man laughs aloud. His laugh rings clear and strange in the still and silent evening. He remembers that he is alone and hushes himself. His sense of loneliness is suddenly acute. Then he imagines the two Israeli soldiers watching him from the ridge. He gets to his feet and quietly leads his cow into the barn.

I have been commended for my marksmanship. When I first joined up, I intended to go into education, so I could stay in the background, where I was used to being. But we all had to complete basic training. We had to be able to carry our kit. We had to learn the *hora* and all the military dances. We had to learn how to dismantle and clean and reassemble whatever weapon had been issued us. We had to learn to shoot. When I have something in my sights, I seem able to hone my concentration down to a still, small point. I kept getting these bull's eyes. My instructors were impressed. It's as if I can be the target. As if my eye and the barrel and what I am aiming for are all just one unified flow of continuity. I wrote home to David about it, and he told me about a book he had read called *Zen and the Art of Archery.* I dropped the education idea. I was increasingly enthusiastic about shooting, and about serving my country. Just because I come from elsewhere doesn't mean that I can't be a patriot. But sometimes I find myself reflecting on my accuracy. I wonder about it. Is it because it's me? Yes, it's because I identify with the target so completely that I am able to nail it. But why should I identify with a shit? I want the shit to be hit, yes. I've no desire to be the shit. And I keep coming back in my mind to my sister and Uncle Sol, and to my brother and what he used to say about his seizures. Could David have been that masked fellahin I brought down the day before yesterday? It's that sort of thought that gives me sleepless nights. Nights when I envy Deborah her snores. Why can't I wake up as her? Then I could get some sleep the following night. And that nurse bitch I hit. At least I can't be her. She is dead. I saw to that. But is this how it works? I can't be sure with these night thoughts. Because, time, perhaps… Perhaps it works backwards as well as forwards. Perhaps I could be Esther in the bible times when next I wake. I need to talk to David about this. Can it be tomorrow that I will be Razan?

I was going up to Huddersfield, to do a poetry reading. Keith was going to meet me at the station. Well, I never got there. And now I am having dreams about poetry readings. Nightmares. Last night, for instance, I dreamt that I was on a large stage, an audience below, about to read my latest work which I had just had published in a chap-book. I put the book down, in order to deliver a preamble about my work – something I very rarely do in wakeful life. I explained that I was going to read poems I had written that made me fear for my safety. My poem about Sergei Skripal, and my poem about being too frightened to read this poem to an audience. This was all very well, but then I just couldn't remember where I had put the chap-book down that I intended to read from. I mumbled on, as I wandered around the stage, surreptitiously glancing here and there, while I tried to locate the chap-book. Very often, in dreams, I arrive at an impasse such as this, and seem to remain suspended in a state that cannot be resolved. That's a phrase you could apply to Israel. And there's another dream that has turned into a nightmare. And is this book in itself a dream that may turn into a nightmare? I've hit upon eighty-four sentences. Each paragraph has to start with one of these sentences and end with another. At some point every sentence that begins a paragraph will be the one that ends another paragraph, while every sentence that concludes a paragraph will also be the start of another paragraph. In this particular paragraph, the one you are reading right now, I have to end with the sentence, I guess I was ten years old. Of course, I could stop here, but that feels like cheating. How do I bring this paragraph, that begins with me travelling up to Huddersfield in my seventies, around to my childhood? What is this fucking book? Is it auto-biography, or is it fiction? Is it a fictive auto-biography? Again, I seem to have hit an impasse. However, in my actions, in my works of performance art, I have learnt that the impasse is the drama. It's not something to wriggle out of. The tension must build up inside the impasse that has been created. Coming back from my pre-prep school on the double-decker bus to the terminus in Shinfield, I used to get into the habit of repeating a phrase to myself, I'm thinking about thinking. This was when I was about five or six. This was perhaps one of my first experiences of an impasse, because I could go on and on, thinking about thinking about thinking, and there seemed to be no way out of what I learnt later was called a regressive series, such as you get when a room has mirrors on walls that face each other. I associate this experience with how thinking about thinking always began just as the bus went over a hump-backed bridge. That was on my way to school. School, I didn't like. Luckily, my widowed mother had a penchant for adventurous holidays, and one year, we set out on a tour, a tour of certain countries in the Middle East, marketed as a tour of the holy land. We visited the Lebanon, and then flew over Syria, landing in Jordan: then, from there, we passed through the Mandelbaum Gate into Israel. Thinking about impasses I have experienced reminds me of the quarry we came across in Baalbek. The builders of one of the greatest temples in the ancient world had carved out of the quarry an immense, rectangular block. But then they hit an impasse. The block was just too heavy to move, to lift, to use elsewhere. And so it's still there, in the quarry, and in some ways it's more impressive than the immense columns that still remain where the great temple once stood, proud and intact. This immovable block made a strong impression on me. I guess I was ten years old.

Life is not a river. Life is not a continuum, whatever Alan Watts has to say about it. We're not here, and then, suddenly, we're here. And then, then we're gone. You think about this sort of stuff, after you've had a seizure or two. It's not just a seizure that presents one with a break in one's continuity. It's birth and death, obviously. And the births and the deaths of the lives that accompany your own. The puppy that suddenly dies in your bed. Or was it a kitten? The death of grand-parents, of children too. The suicides. The death of those you hate as well as those you love. Life is not a river, and neither is your family a tree, and neither is your race any sort of legacy. The genetic make-up of the people inhabiting Jerusalem before the rebellion against Rome in 70 A.D. cannot be traced to contemporary persons who happen to adhere to Judaism. Josephus claims that 1,100,000 people were killed during the siege of Jerusalem, so therefore the expulsion was more of a holocaust than a dispersal. Despite "authentic" Jewish ancestry being dependent on the matrilineal line (since the males often consorted with their non-Jewish concubines) every family has its cupboards packed with skeletons. This is as true for those who practise Judaism as it is for Nigerians. And of course it holds true for aristocracies, which must include the supposed lineage of the British Royal Family. Where it is not the case, hybrid vigour sets in, as my veterinary mother explained – when filling out the pedigree for our dalmatians if they were to be mated. It's not good for the species to be mated with those who are too closely related – as when pharaohs or Roman emperors marry their sisters and Hapsburgs marry their cousins. Hyper-kinship results in infertility, seizures, imbecility, prognathism and hare-lips. No race flows down through history like some uninterrupted river that rejects every tributary. To equate race with religion is essentially a false premise. A great Arabic Queen called Hind converted to Christianity, when she found it expedient to do so, in the century before the birth of Mohamed. Many believe that the Russian Khazars converted to Judaism in the ninth century, and these are the ancestors of today's Ashkenazi Jews. Arthur Koestler's best-selling *The Thirteenth Tribe* (1976) brought this story to the attention of Western audiences; the book's central thesis being that East European Ashkenazi Jewry was largely of Khazar origin. Shaul Stampfer, Rabbi Edward Sandrow Professor of Soviet and East European Jewry and chairman of the Department of Jewish History at the Hebrew University of Jerusalem goes to very great lengths to dispute this claim, for, as he says "the view that some or all of the Khazars became Jews lends credence to claims that the bulk of East European Jewry was not descended from *ethnic* Jews. This carries political implications with regard to the ties between contemporary Jews and the Land of Israel. There are those who see religious and other consequences if contemporary Jewry can be shown *not* to be descended from the Israelites described in the Bible." Well, however much the learned professor may protest, an "ethnic" claim to Palestine by those who often profess to practise Judaism is not borne out by genetics, nor by contemporary studies. Sadly, to my mind, I don't see how Judaism can survive established Zionism. Judaism is a faith in which the spiritual notion of exile (which originates in our expulsion from the Garden of Eden) will ultimately be reunited with the home of its soul in the all-embracing Kingdom, on the Final Day. Zionism is an atheist-originated, illusory belief in racial superiority and the right to appropriate property and territory conferred by a very dodgy interpretation of history. My history teacher once pointed out to me that family trees should be uprooted and stood on their heads. Each of our parents had two parents, each of these four grandparents had two parents. Our genetic ancestry expands as we go back in time, which means, as he put it, that we are all descended from William the Conqueror. Why do I make such a fuss about this? Perhaps because in Judaic terms, I am not considered a Jew. It doesn't count that my father was one. When I visited Israel with my mother in 1954, I was not returning to the land of my ancestors. I was just a boy, curious about archaeology, brought up by an atheist mum. My father had been a socialist who rejected his father's Zionist aims. I wore sandals. On the road to the Dead Sea, I bargained with a nomad boy for his sling. In the old city of Jerusalem, part of the Kingdom of Jordan in those days, another boy befriended me. He took me all over his city, which was, it seemed, still part of the Middle Ages. Winding alleys, houses with open rooves leading by steps to other houses with open rooves. We threaded our way through these alleys and then through the bazaars. My hair was cut short in the smartest of schoolboy crops. I was to meet my Uncle Felix the following day, after we had passed through the Mandelbaum Gate, which I thought of as gate so small a camel would have to pass through it on its knees. The Eye of the Needle. I wore khaki shorts. I had this zip-up wind-cheater jacket: it had an elasticated waist.

At eighteen, she left everything behind to fulfil her dream of living in Israel. This was the land where she belonged. She had never felt that she belonged in Boston. But then, back there, being white, she had felt like a thief. Wasn't the Shawmut Peninsula originally connected to the mainland to its south by a narrow isthmus and surrounded by an estuary of the river? Back then it wasn't called the Charles. It had that native American name. And hadn't excavations conducted during the construction of buildings and subways in the city shown that this peninsula was inhabited as early as 7,500 years before her time? Prior to the arrival of European colonists on the eastern shore of New England, the area around Massachusetts Bay was the territory of several Algonquian-speaking tribes: the Massachusett, the Nauset and the Wampanoag. The Pennacooks occupied the Merrimack River valley to the north, and the Nipmuc, Pocumtuc and Mahican people occupied the western lands, although some of those tribes were already under tribute to the Mohawks, who were expanding aggressively from upstate New York. Becca learnt all this in school. It sickened her. At school, she a friend who had Pocumtuc blood in her. She told Becca what her grandparents had told her parents. The colonists had just ridden into Massachusetts and stolen everything from the peoples whose land it was. They brought with them a pestilence that killed as many as two-thirds of the indigenous population. Land divisions between the tribes had been well understood and respected. The colonists just grabbed all they could, which was everything. Becca had no wish to be an accomplice after this fact. Somewhere, in the depths of her childhood, she knew that she had been the one from whom everything had been taken. After several mishaps with young men, she turned to the synagogue and became so devout she got on the nerves of her own family. Then a young rabbi called David introduced her to more up-to-date ideas. There was no reason whatsoever why the promised land should remain a merely symbolic entity, realised only on the Day of Judgement. Uncle Sol backed up the words of the rabbi. It was perfectly possible for Becca to apply for citizenship of her own country. She could start by going to work on a kibbutz. Being in the country as of right and not on sufferance.

Can things happen to you that you simply have no recollection of, things that you just can't remember? Like the times your Uncle Sol took you both along to those parties at the army camp. These times are like dreams. Their narratives seem to fade as you wake up from them. But why do you feel so sore down below? As if you had developed a rash or something. And sometimes there is a rash, and it lasts and it lasts, and it doesn't go away, but for some reason you are too ashamed to tell Mum about it. Because. Although you tingle there, you can't remember anything happening. It's not as if you went into the bushes and did something with other kids, like you used to get spanked for, when you were just a kid yourself. That you remember. And the spanking. And the spanking…yes. Probably it's because, well, you don't want to remember. Becca woke after sleeping fitfully most of the night. It was too hot to sleep comfortably. In the dormitory of the barracks there were other girls tossing and turning. She looked across to the bed next to her, where her friend Deborah was sleeping. Was she awake? If she were awake, they could go outside and have a smoke together. Deborah seemed to be dead to the world. Lucky bitch. She was almost always able to sleep really well. Deborah said she never dreamt at all. You're so fucking lucky, bitch. Deborah would snore. Now Rebecca thought back to one of their last conversations. I have dreams, I know I do. In my sleep I know I'm there in the middle of whatever's going on, going on in the dream, I mean. I just tend to lose it when I get out of bed. Deborah was a pal. One of the few women with whom Rebecca got along. Like Rebecca, she was a sharp-shooter. They would train on the ranges together. She was one tough bitch. Built like a tank. A hockey ace. You I get along with, normally I don't, Becca told her once. Not with girls, I mean. They act like they could feel ashamed about things, I mean, like they're all coy and respectable. Or that's what they project. But what I've noticed is, they feel no fucking guilt. No guilt at all, if you get what I mean. A girl will keep her tits secure, in the tightest bra. Sure, but she'll steal your boyfriend off you. Your boyfriend or…Becca let the sentence drop. Then she went on, she'll diss you to command, so that she gets the promotion you were after. Deborah would nod her head. She had a short, thick neck. Becca, you're right about that. Girls are shit. I used to aim for the men, but now I aim for the girls.

Like the times your Uncle Sol took you both along to those parties at the army camp. That was back in Massachusetts. How old had you been? Ten? When it began, that is…before your sister joined in. Well, eleven maybe. Yes, but it's hidden away so well it's very hard to know. Now we're going to treat you like a real grown-up, Rebecca. Where was this getting her? Why did the clouds roll in here, moving across memories, obliterating fixtures in their landscape like a fog? Like a fog, or not. Was it simply what she wouldn't say, wouldn't ever admit? But what was it that she wouldn't ever admit? Trouble was, it wasn't simple. There was her sister. And then, it hadn't just been her uncle. Her aunt had been there. And there had been pain, yes, of that she was pretty sure. But what she could never ever say, even to herself, was that there had been, or there may have been. As well as pain…its opposite. But that was way back when, when she had only been Rebecca, back in the Boston days. Back before she had gotten tough. How good it had been to have driven off all that shame, all that letting them do it, all that filthy stuff: driven it out of her, here in Eretz Israel. Here, where you didn't have to go naked into iniquity, into the showers that never rain. Israel had taught her *not* to be a victim. We're the tough guys here, Deborah would say. We're not the sheep, we're the hounds. The wolves. We're the guards this time. Better to be bullies than to cower. Becca, look, you gotta toughen up. Like me. I'm not gonna be Deborah any more. I am gonna be Daniel. I am gonna fuck with the lions. They had laughed. And it was after this that Rebecca began to think of herself as Yehuda, or better still, Adonai. Yeah, the Lord himself. And so they got into the way of calling each other by their male names. Deborah knew her own myths. And she told Rebecca, look, here we're the masters. Here we are the master-race. Here, it's us. Here, in the land of milk and honey, we have instituted the Fourth Reich.

Sergei Skripal turns out to have been
Christopher Steele's associate.
During the presidential elections,
They had worked together on a dossier
Laced with detrimental footage

Russian operatives allegedly
Had to dish on Donald Trump.
Steele was MI6. An adept officer,
Under diplomatic cover, he was operant
In Russia and in Paris, and at the FO.

After he quit the service, though
A pillar of that secretive establishment,
He supplied the FBI with evidence
Of bribery at FIFA: sterling work
On international soccer that lent credence

To his material on Trump's entanglements.
Colourful these. Trump hiring prostitutes
To piss on a bed that Barack
And Michelle were said to have slept in
In the Moscow Ritz Carlton.

This, I maintain, is the poem that had got me into trouble. I published it on Facebook and on my blog, shortly after the Russian Embassy staff were expelled. It was just a few days before I set out for Huddersfield. I was lucky. My pre-booked seat was one with a table in front of it. Most of the seats just faced the back of the seats in front of them. A rather lovely girl was already sitting diagonally across from me. Long, dark hair. I kept trying to glance at her and not look as if I was doing it. As you get older, you get better at that. She was slim, restless. A larger, older woman, came and sat beside me, and I seem to remember red hair. I think she smiled at me as she took her seat, willing to be amicable. The express to Leeds pulled out of King's Cross. Very quickly, we gathered speed. Lightning speed. Stations took no more than an instant to flash past. Who would have wanted me dead? Not Trump, for if I was right, it's clear that some element of the Secret Services was working against his campaign, rather than colluding with it. More likely his enemies. None of this was in my mind as we whizzed on up to Leeds. I was happy with the small bottle of Ribena I had purchased before boarding, and I wanted to read. What was the book? The book escapes me. It was then that the train suddenly slowed down and came to a stop. Nothing got switched off. It was as if we were being held back by our brakes alone. The whole carriage was shuddering. One felt the electricity surging on through the rails below the carriage. "We are being held here, because the train ahead of us has been in collision with an object." At this, we all glanced at each other. A body? A cow? The whole train continued to vibrate. "What do you think it's collided with?" I asked the buxom lady with the red hair. She smiled and shrugged. Now was the time to get on with my book. I reached into my breast pocket for my spectacles. I fumbled with them and they dropped beneath my seat. This was both irritating and inconvenient. My seat was too close to the edge of the table for me to reach down. I had to stand and ask the woman next to me to get up and move out of her seat while I knelt down underneath the table, in order to retrieve my spectacles. I was making quite a spectacle of myself. The space was cramped, dark, vibrating, just above the immense voltage that was on the surge below the floor of the carriage. I secured my spectacles. I thanked the buxom lady profusely as I re-installed myself in my seat. I opened my book, but felt sleepy actually, and so I leant my head against the frame of the window, in order to have a little snooze. It was then that she must have struck, that is, as I drifted off, and I think she pricked my left hand, the hand that was closest to her, between my little finger and its neighbour. It was there, later, that I discerned the shadow of a bruise. Was she an agent of Mossad? Becca tells me I am far too small a fry for them to bother about the poems I may write. I have to admit that I can see the sense in what she says. I am not that important in the scheme of things. Ok, so perhaps I should abandon my far-fetched theories. I've just gone epileptic in my dotage. There was that event last year, when obviously I was unable to find the lavatory door. Leo, one of my great uncles on the Jewish side, seems to have suffered from seizures.

He has been born again, as a girl called Rebecca. That's how it is, when you conk out. You come to, yes, but are you the you you were before you conked out? How do you know that you are? Yes, you are a you that feels intact, that is, you have all the memories, you sense a continuity in yourself that goes back to the day you were born. But that is all being experienced in the now of who you are now. There is only the present, after all. And now she is Rebecca, but, before the jeep overturned and she conked out, she could have been him. Who? Well, she could have been anyone, even someone of the opposite sex. Increasingly, in actual fact, Rebecca has been feeling like a man. She has even given him, that is, the man she is, a name. Adonai. A lordly name. As she brings her palms together and uses dynamic tension to intensify her pectorals she will chant in her mind, I am I, Ad-on-Ai. Sometimes, she feels wrong to be calling herself by this name. She is a girl, not God. When she senses this, she uses Yehuda instead. Trouble is, there are already two Yehudas in her squad. Or there were. One of them has a mantra. Hit back twice as hard.

The sixty years and more that he carried on his shoulders had not bent his back. He remained erect and alert, for he belonged to that sort of men whose age shows only in their white hair and the few wrinkles of their faces.

One could hardly have supposed him more than forty, on seeing him walking to the field, followed by his cow.

When he reaches the field, he tethers the cow, takes his shovel in his hands and gets to work. He intends to dig round the roots of the vines as he does every year at this time. Trees are like children; they need love and care to grow strong.

The sun is already high above the horizon when he finishes with the last vine. He had started the task some days ago when Hassan Saleh was still there. But Hassan could not be induced to work, he would only sit in the shade of that tree, watching Idriss dig and talking all the while.

From time to time, when he was bored with digging round the vines, Idriss would consider the ditch, to which he now turns to give this task his full attention. The day before, he had stopped digging when he reached a small rock which was preventing the water from reaching that nut tree. If he could only get the water to the tree he could plant tomatoes in its shade. A tomato would be good, here on any autumn day.

But how to be rid of this accursed rock? Of course, he could simply dig around it, but when yesterday he had determined to break it, he'd assumed that the matter was simple and that the task was going to be easy.

Now, however, an hour passes before he realizes he can do nothing and that he's trying to break the rock in vain. But this will not discourage him. Better toil on, and eventually rid the ground of it than allow it to keep standing there. The land it occupies can be used to altogether better ends.

Digging all around this obstacle, he manages to wedge his axe underneath it, puts a stone under the shaft and bears down on the handle now with all his weight. He hears a crack which makes him stop, he fears the shaft will snap. He tries to shake the rock to and fro', using his bare hands.

Now he can't avoid thinking of Hassan Saleh and how he would have ridiculed his efforts, were he there. He would certainly have laughed aloud, and pretty hard, baring his toothless gums, his eyes filling with tears. This used to happen whenever Hassan caught him doing something at which he was unlikely to succeed.

Stop exerting yourself, Idriss. Look, you're growing old. Leave the business to one who is younger. As for you, your time is up.

Not my time but yours is up!

Don't be stubborn, man. You're worn out by an hour's work. Come. Sit down and take it easy. You won't carry anything with you, you know, beyond the blessed grave.

Do you suppose I'm working here just to open an account?

But why tire yourself out? You've got enough to eat.

I swear I never work merely out of a greed for it. But, still, it's a shame to leave this earth here idle.

Why then are you always so concerned when there's a meagre crop?

Because I prefer not to see my labour wasted. Planting is like giving birth. Would you be contented for your wife to have a miscarriage?

Hassan Saleh used to laugh so mockingly:

Ah, so that's why you're so busy!

I swear on the prophet's grave, I never leave off working just because I'm tired. I leave off... because I've had enough. Just as one can have enough of eating or of a woman even.

Hassan went on laughing, of course. They all used to laugh at him when Idriss talked with vehemence about his work on the land. How was he to make them understand him properly?

Shaking off his daydream now, he looks around him. Here he is, alone, hands and face moist with perspiration. A vague feeling that those two soldiers are out there watching him seizes hold of his heart. Idriss half expects to meet their eyes. He looks towards the distant ridge, mechanically wiping his brow with the back of his sleeve. Nothing but empty country.

That soldier told me they were there; but I can't believe he would actually give away their position. It is not like a soldier simply to show you his camp. Let him laugh as loud as he likes, though what's there to laugh at? Nothing.

Having made sure that his cow is contentedly chewing her cud, he goes back to tackling the stone.

In children's tales a trove is found, underneath so difficult a rock.

His arms and shoulders ache.

Hamed would have helped, if he were here. He is young and could prise it loose alone, without much help from me.

He stops trying and sits down in the shade of the nut-tree to roll a cigarette. The sun blazes down on him as he gazes now at the land and now at his cow. In his mind he sees the land throbbing with heat. It could be the bosom of a pregnant woman. Where does fertility come from? Why is one piece of this earth as different from another as women are different from each other? Idriss remembers what he used to tell his son: the land is like a woman in need of a man. The land will give that man plenty, of course. But, like a woman, that land must be cared for. If we don't sweat and toil over it, it can betray and neglect us, or, at the least, not give us our bread.

His eyes roam over the distant fields; a vague emotion grips him and he feels a lump in his throat. The fields are covered thickly with wheat stalks, most of them empty. A year ago, the war had come before harvest time. Most of the country people had not been able to reap their fields. The ripened grain fell to the earth in Autumn – to grow plentifully but without purpose the following Spring.

The village itself is empty now. Idriss looks towards it with a mixture of incomprehension and despair. Why did the Jews leave him here and not chase him out or put an end to him?

Is it because they think I can do them no harm? Or do they have something in store for me?

He cannot accept the idea that he has been spared because they consider him harmless. And so he is somehow gratified to see a military jeep come jolting through the village. He is pretty sure they are coming for him.

The jeep stops a few yards across from him and a youngish face appears to be beckoning to him.

The military Governor wants to see you at Qneitra.

To see me?

Yes, you.

What does he want from me? Can't you see I'm busy?

I don't know what it's about. He just told us to bring you to him. No need to be scared.

I fear God alone. But right now I'm busy here. I'm not ready to go.

He also told us to bring you by force if you refused… to come of your own accord.

By force? And who can force me? You? You just come and try.

Saying this, Idriss grips the handle of his shovel very tightly.

The young soldier gets off the jeep and approaches him, smiling and cordial enough.

Look, nobody's going to use force! But your presence at Qneitra is urgently required. Maybe be they want to give you a letter, or a parcel somebody has sent to you from Damascus.

From Damascus?

Yes, through the International Red Cross.

Wait a moment then, says the old man in a more conciliatory tone. I am just going to give the cow more length to her tether, and then I will go with you.

Idriss goes towards the house and comes back with a long rope. He attaches one end to the horns of the cow and the other to the nut-tree. Smiling still, the young soldier looks on.

That is pretty useless, aren't you afraid your cow will run off?

No, but she might well damage the plants.

A sly expression appears on the face of the soldier, which reminds Idriss of the mocking laughter of those other two Israelis. Anxious now, he looks at the cow and then looks at the soldier.

What if she is stolen?

Don't worry, nothing's going to keep you from your cow.

The smooth manner of the one he is speaking with astonishes him. Idriss expected coarser language. He seats himself in the back seat of the jeep while the soldier occupies the seat in front, next to the driver.

Are you alone in the village? the driver inquires.

Yes… I'm alone.

Why didn't you leave?

Where am I to go?

Where everybody else has gone.

Whatever for? Here, I am at home. Anyway, the others will be back.

The driver laughs and speaks to his companion in their strange language.

Do you really think that they'll be back? he asks.

Certainly! I see no reason why not. They will come back to their homes. How could it possibly be that they should have left their homes and property for ever?

Aha, how optimistically you listen to those songs, the ones broadcast daily by Damascus.

For a few turns of the wheel, Idriss remains quiet, thinking hard.

How is it that he has never faced it, the thought they might never return? Ah, but to whom did they leave these fields for which they have toiled and disputed?

Now the laugh of these two Israelis drags him out of his deeper thoughts.

We are victorious. Aren't you aware of it? We have defeated all your Arab armies.

What do you mean?

That we have taken possession – of your territory. From Syria, from Egypt, and from Jordan too.

Taken it?

Man, don't you know it yet?

I know that your army came into Qneitra. But to say that this entitles you to take possession of the land...

It comes down to the same thing. To say that an army reached such land means that it has taken it.

You haven't taken my land from me.

Not only your land, but, from now on, I guess, you yourself belong to us.

*Idriss swears in Arabic. The two soldiers try to repeat the words
they haven't yet been taught.*

I have not been defeated, Idriss says at last.

All your people have.

But I stay on and the land shall remain my own.

*As the jeep draws nearer to Qneitra, the great memorial appears
in the distance. One day, two years ago, Idriss had stopped there to look at
a big crowd gathered round this monument. He had then inquired from
one of them:*

What is going on here?

This is the tomb of the unknown soldier!

*What? Are they burying him now? Didn't they know who his
parents were?*

*No, man. This is only a symbol. It stands for all the soldiers who
have died defending our land.*

Why are so many gathered here?

*A dignitary is just about to lay a wreath on the tomb. This rep-
resents a homage to all the soldiers who have died on the field of battle.
Listen to the bugle now.*

*The bugle sounded melancholy in its own eerie way that day,
when Idriss had compared it to a lament for his country. How many
soldiers had died in the hostilities, before the enemy managed to reach
Qneitra? The jeep he sat in now sped past the memorial, moving too fast
for him to see if there were flowers on its tomb.*

There was a nurse with her hands in the air approaching the fence.
The fence at that point was about twelve feet high. Its concrete pillars
then inclined away from Israel, like hockey sticks, taking the fence
up a further three feet. Some shit was prostrate but calling out next
to the fence on the Gaza side. The nurse in her red head-scarf was

approaching him slowly, fully aware that she was in range. The shit was screaming, rather than calling out. Through her sights, Rebecca could just make out the blood. It was soaking his trousers close to the waist. She guessed it was Yehuda's shot. He never aimed for the head. To Rebecca's mind, by not aiming so as to finish a shit off from the start, Yehuda lost sight of his aim. Their aim. That aim was to wipe their homeland clear of all that which was not authentic, not kosher, not spawned of the Lion of Judah. When he shot to maim, he missed the point. The point was to be accurate, and to achieve your aim. This was the Promised Land. This was the soil of their fathers. Generation after generation had been buried here, back in the old days. You could say this soil was made of her ancestors and of Yehuda's ancestors. This she felt very strongly. After all, she had never bonded with Boston, although she just happened to have been born there. But that first day on the Kibbutz, seven years ago now, when David had picked her an orange, an orange off a tree another Kibbutznik had planted. Then she had felt it. Then. Her finger curled around the trigger. Focus, she told herself. Aim. So that it should not enter your mind that the heavens and all their host and the earth and all it contains are separate entities in themselves.

He learnt later that her name was Razan. She was a first-response nurse, on the Palestinian side of the fence. She was wearing a red head-scarf and the white coat of a medical orderly. She and some other medics were walking with their hands in the air and they all looked glaringly white, wearing their white coats as they approached the border fence in order to treat a wounded offender. A day after her death, he watched footage released by the IDF in which she openly admitted to participating in the offences as a human shield, at the request of Hamas. He felt the fury rising in his throat. Women were always the worst. Hadn't Miriam fucked Richard behind her back, in the grim days back in Boston when she was still Rebecca? Hadn't Hava gone with Uncle Sol? And as for this shit bitch, the footage proved he was right to have pulled the trigger. What was Hamas but a terrorist outfit, a gang, corruptly ruling over Gaza, just like any mafia that rules over its fiefdom? Wasn't Hamas always camouflaging its own misdemeanours by calling for Israel to be annulled, its people to be driven into the sea? It reminded what remained of Rebecca in him of a poem she had found on her uncle's bookshelf, the ending, that is, of a poem called *Eros Turannos,* by an old-fashioned git called Arlington Robinson:

> Meanwhile we do no harm; for they
> That with a god have striven,
> Not hearing much of what we say,
> Take what the god has given;
> Though like waves breaking it may be,
> Or like a changed familiar tree,
> Or like a stairway to the sea
> Where down the blind are driven.

It was as if Hamas were comparing Israel to Sodom, the bastards. Sodom, struck with blindness.

She felt so fab as Yehuda in her uniform. Especially in the green, black and brown of her camouflage. It was cool how the camouflage webbing fitted so neatly over her helmet. Her far wider mitznefet was even cooler. It was like an extravagantly large beret, washed over by a green ocean featuring cloud islets of black, grey, brown and yellow. A war bonnet, proudly to be worn by warriors of either sex. Kitted out in her camouflage, she felt all the more how she had become Yehuda, how she had to become him. Sometimes, on her free afternoon, she wouldn't leave the barracks. She would wait until the others had gone out clubbing. Then she would just switch kits. This was back at the barracks outside Haifa. There was an orderly's room in the block in front of the lavatories where David had been found hanging. There was a full-length mirror in it. When she could get away with it, she would sneak in there with her kit-bag. She'd put on her NVG goggles, slip into her TV711 tactical combat vest, fit to her hydration tube her camo hydration tube cover that neatly covered her camelback source thermoback Blackhawk bladder in OD Green. After that, she would strap on her black knee-pads. But whenever she strapped these to her knees she just couldn't help thinking about kneeling, like the shits knelt sometimes before they got knocked off. Should she fit them to her knees before kneeling before her commanding officer? Sucking off his tube… The silly phrase just came to her. But would Yehuda fit them to his knees before kneeling before his commanding officer? Would she ever get to command Yehuda? The changes rung by her kit brought out all these weird day-dream phrases. And so it was seriously necessary to concentrate on the mirror. Fix the eyes there. Try on the drop-leg holster, fit her G17 pistol into it, get into the groove, just as the others were getting into it at the club, hitting the speed. But not dancing to Shakira, because Shakira wasn't played any more. Fitting the weapon together, quickening her reflexes, getting the drill correct, down to the last iota. Hup, click, hip. Carbine, reflex sight with mount, mag-holder, fuck, assemble, dismantle, assemble, dissemble, dissemble. Make out what a great mitzvah and an honour it was to serve as a religious soldier. Born again in the IDF, born again as Yehuda. Here to make Aliyah in order to defend the state. Walk in the steps of Jehovah as he walks the earth. Now. Now that she can't just go on being Rebecca, not the Rebecca, that is, who was just so dumb and stupid about men, back in Boston. It's better to be Yehuda. After all the training, she doesn't even have Rebecca's body any more. She is not the plump, gun-shy girl she once might have been. Once, but never again. There is no continuity.

The hunt was on for mushrooms. And so I dug my heels into Dusty's sides. Katie's piebald began to canter and that made Dusty break into a gallop. Dusty was faster than her piebald. And a better jumper. But Katie was a better rider than me. She used to borrow Dusty and win rosettes at gymkhanas on him. One mushroom and we'd win the treasure hunt. We'd already found everything else on the list. We raced beneath the oaks. I kept my eyes on the ground. Bracken. Gorse. The roots of a….blond. I went blond for a while. After Richard left me for Miriam. But you have to keep doing it. Otherwise it shows through at the roots, especially when your hair is as dark as mine. And it didn't help me to forget Richard. Or how I felt, what I wanted to happen, to happen to Miriam. Up until then, we had been best friends. Not to mention Hava. Miriam, you know, she used to feel ashamed that her fingers were all stubby. Most of the girls would tease her for having stubby, unsightly fingers. It was because she bit her nails. The bitch. She bit them for ages, after we left school, I mean. I expect she still bites them. I bet Richard teases her about it. She felt ashamed of biting them, but not of stealing Richard off me. Girls feel more shame than boys, but they never seem to feel guilt. I loved Richard. He was a Goy, but so lovely and under-standing and open-minded about everything. I guess I wasn't quite so open-minded. Miriam was though. The bitch. I felt like a snail whose horns have been hit. I went back into my family as if it were a shell. But then there were memories… Hava…who is married now.

And memories of Uncle Sol. There was a young rabbi I quite liked, and so, for a while, I became a Jewy sort of Jew. I became an ultra-yid. But then Miriam and Richard got married. Boston just began to stink. Boston stank of Miriam and Richard. I pestered Uncle Sol, and he sent me on a visit, back to the Promised Land. I worked for a year on a kibbutz. There was a boy there I liked, but he got shot while harvesting the oranges. I learnt to love a state. I gave up on people. Fell in love with Eretz Israel. I learned to loathe the shits. I joined the Israeli Defence Force as a soldier specialising in education, but later I decided that I was meant for the field.

You're pulling my leg. No, mate, I am not pulling your leg. You kept on saying, That's my Ribena, that's my Ribena. The ambulance man's head is very close to mine. I can see trees, an avenue of trees, on either side of the road we are leaving behind. I can see these trees through the double windows of the ambulance's rear door. I am horizontal. The road is bumpy, or so it seems to me. It feels like a country road. We're rattling, we're shuddering. Know this day and take it into your heart.

From December, 1923, through January, 1925, I directed the Keren haYesod activities in Austria. And from the very first day I was at odds with the leading Austrian Zionists, including even my good friend Robert Strieker, concerning the basic tithe principle to which I thought we should invariably adhere. In their opinion, the main task was to get some sort of contribution from every Jew. They felt that anyone who gave the equivalent of one-pound sterling, no matter what his means, should be considered as having fulfilled his duty. The obvious but nonetheless very disappointing result was that we did not make much financial headway among the Zionists of Austria.

Nor did we manage to get their effective co-operation in our efforts to win leading non-Zionists to accept the idea of the Jewish National Home. There were exceptions. One notable sympathizer with our cause was Dr. Sigmund Freud, whom friend Strieker and I went to visit. He was eager to learn all about our plans for the development of the Jewish National Home, and we had a long talk with him. Though he told us that the state of his health would not permit him to attend any of our functions, he did authorize us to mention—whenever we thought it might be helpful for our cause—that he took an active and sympathetic interest in the activities of the Keren haYesod. There were two occasions on which we succeeded in getting generous response from affluent non-Zionists and even anti-Zionists in Vienna. The first occurred when Dr. Albert Einstein graciously consented to interrupt a trip he was taking to Italy in order to speak at a K.H. meeting in Vienna. The magic spell of his name induced a number of prominent Jewish businessmen who had never before attended a pro-Palestine function to forget their prejudices for this one night. Professor Einstein spoke very forthrightly, and his listeners did not particularly like what he said, but they nonetheless contributed quite generously to the Fund when we visited them in their offices the next morning. The second successful meeting of this kind was held in the home of one of the most prominent members of society. Present were a large number of wealthy Jewish bankers and businessmen. Our speaker was my old friend Dr. Nahum Goldmann. The lively discussion that followed his brilliant address continued into the wee hours after midnight. There were all the usual objections, and dozens of questions had to be answered by Dr. Goldmann. At the very end, one particularly stubborn member of the audience had this to say: "All that you pointed out, Dr. Goldmann, may be true," he conceded. "Yet even so your experiment is bound to fail, since the decisive element that would ensure success is missing. History has shown that Australia and other frontier countries were colonized successfully only because the people who did the pioneering work were desperadoes, criminals, men for whom there was no bridge on which to return to the homeland. They had no choice but to stick to the task before them. Your pioneers, on the other hand, have come from countries where they were clerks and students, workers and artisans. They have come of their own free will driven by an ideal, but many of them will not be able to cope with the difficulties that they are bound to meet. For them, return to their homelands will be quite possible. They are not the element you need to ensure your success." With his most disarming smile, Dr. Goldmann countered: "Please do not worry about the spirit and the energy of our chalutzim. They are all right. But there is indeed an element of truth in what you say. It is quite correct that thus far we have made headway among certain strata of our people only—the workers, the intellectuals, the small middle-class people who have responded affirmatively to our message. We have not yet reached the one element that has already burned the bridges to its past, and that by its reckless energy and unfettered ability to use its elbows has ascended to a higher level of society. This, gentlemen, is why we now appeal to you." The targets of his wily barb took it in good part. Some, it seemed to me, even felt flattered.

Some, it seemed to him, even felt flattered. Flattered to be compared to desperadoes, criminals. And that's how I remember childhood. It was not just a matter of being a cowboy. It was great to be outside the law and to wear a scarf around the nose. When I grow up, well, I want to be a desperado. At least I do at the age of seven. I have learnt to steal. And I have learnt only to steal from my mother. She never seems to notice that I've been inside her bag. Once I stole from my grandmother. Once, and never again. We were on a visit to her house in Alma Terrace, Kensington. I went out into the street and impressed the cockneys with my new gun. My grandmother came storming after me. Anthony, you've stolen from my bag. She scolded me directly, there in the street, in front of the boys I was ever so keen to impress. I never cared to play with them again. I never dared. From then on, I only stole from Mum. I graduated from stealing around the age of eleven or twelve. By then I think it was sex that mostly occupied my mind. I am quite certain though that I was never in love with Katie, but she was quite certainly in love with my pony. That's the Gospel Truth. I never thought of my pony as a pony though. Steeldust was a horse. Though he had been a polo pony. That's how he had been schooled at least. You could guide him with one hand. He understood. If, with one hand, you let him feel the rein to the right on his neck, he would turn towards the left. That left you a hand free. There was a casual ease about it. It was a dandy way to ride. Dusty was great at dressage. He jumped very neatly as well. We were both such keen huntsmen that we were made honorary whippers-in. I can remember banging my crop against my boot, to deter the fox from leaving a field of Kale. But Katie loved dressage. She loved to come to our paddocks and school Dusty. In retrospect, I realise I could have got more out of her. Probably. Got to have touched her somewhere in return for letting her school my lovely horse. But this feels like a fantasy. Of that I am sure. Maybe I knew her too well. Her mum and mine were best friends. They had both been at the Royal Veterinary College – Katie's mother in the year above Deborah's. That was the very first year that women were admitted into the college. Katie's mum was a pioneer. And maybe it was also because Katie mainly got to school Dusty when I went over to her place. I wasn't on familiar soil. I don't recall thinking about her in a horny way. I felt horny about plenty of other girls, and about plenty of boys. But we were as close as brothers and sisters, and that can take the glamour out of such situations as one finds oneself in, as is not made clear by much erotica. Katie was a rider, a truly serious rider. We went to gymkhanas and pony club camps together. Once we teamed up for a treasure hunt. She had a pretty piebald by then. Not so good at dressage as Dusty, but very fast on her hooves. The idea was, we were to collect a number of things and bring them back to the base: an oakleaf, a mushroom, some bracken, a spray of broom. Things easy enough to acquire on Burghfield or Bucklebury Common. I can't quite remember which common it was. The first team back at the base with all the items won the hunt. Sometimes Katie followed me, at other times I followed her. Her horse went hell-for-leather across the common.

Idriss is introduced into the Governor's office. The Governor greets him affably enough and requests those present to leave them alone. As they file out, Idriss notices curious smiles on their faces.

The Governor now begins to speak with a certain touch of irony in his voice.

And your cow, Idriss al Akhdir, is she doing well?

Idriss is taken aback. He wasn't expecting the Governor to use his name. And how does he know about my cow and what interest is she to him? And so he answers with some defiance, as if the inquiry was about a real person.

She wishes you the best, thank you!

You are exactly as I thought you would be, Idriss. Now, listen to me.

The Governor adopts a serious tone, while Idriss is thinking, the son of a bitch. He even calls me, Idriss!

The Governor goes on:

All the people of your village have left but you stay on alone. You are not being especially prudent. Somebody might kill you… trying to steal your cow. Your body might well rot before we could be made aware of what has happened to you.

Why all this, this beating the bush? What are you aiming at actually?

I simply want to give you some advice. Why don't you get packed and go away?

Go away, and leave the village?

Yes, why not? You're free to take your cow along with you. Unless you prefer to sell her. I can find someone who would buy her for… five hundred Syrian pounds. As you see we are not without a heart. We can… even be friends.

No. No, we can't.

You refuse our friendship?

Since the Governor says this in a reproachful tone, the old man begins to feel embarrassed. The situation is awkward. Idriss prefers to remain silent.

Anyway, I didn't ask you to come here to talk about friendship. You need to decide about your cow to-day!

No.

This is my advice to you, although I do realise that I'm no older than your son. Sell the cow and get away.

Years ago, Idriss had been once called to a police station. The sight of a policeman had always been enough to unsettle him. But now he is not afraid. He is going to maintain his dignity in front of this foreigner, who must not be allowed to take advantage of him, or to take him for a fool.

Now, what have you decided?

About what?

About your blessed cow. Are you going to sell? I am pretty sure she's worth no more than what I've offered you.

Lord, how stupid this Governor bastard is being. Unless he is acting stupid. As though the cow were the only snag. Even were I to accept his price, why should I have to pack up and go?

I am not selling my cow.

You do realise that we can do whatever we like, by force if necessary. It's only your age that makes us patient with you, Idriss. Let me once more advise you to get out.

Where can I go?

To Damascus, just like all the others.

The others will be back. Soon, they will be back.

Now, let me explain. And you must understand this once and for all. We are not going to permit anyone to come back. If we had wanted them here we would not have chased them off. You must have noticed how harsh our soldiers have been, with the village. What can we do? This is war! As for you, I don't think anyone yet has molested you. Clearly you are a wise, brave old fellow. But look, we need Mansura and some other villages. None of their former inhabitants are going to be permitted to return. The forces of Eretz-Israel intend to remain on this occupied soil!

What has my cow to do with this?

The Governor sighs.

We only want to warn you that you mustn't wait for anyone to come back anymore. You need to go, get out. We'll try to find a buyer for your cow! Now you must admit, no other troops behave this way in a war.

And the land? I sense that you continually forget about the land, the land itself.

You go beyond all limits on our patience, that's the truth! We're not going to buy your taken land.

Idriss considers this reply an insult. He feels cold in the back.

I am not telling you this because I want to sell. Far from it. But I want you to understand that, if I stay on, it's not because of the cow but because of the land. You know the one completes the other, man. How do I plough my fields if I sell the cow? I'm even considering... the purchase of a second cow.

We simply haven't time for all this chattering.

This land is mine and not your father's. All my life I've spent on it. I will not go away, and my cow is not for sale.

For a brief moment, the Governor stands amused at the stubbornness of this old man. He's let him speak his mind, and he still hesitates to give the conversation a sharper tone.

Try to understand me, Idriss. Don't force me into coming down hard. We need to set up a Kibbutz in your village. Work on this will start in a few days' time. You can, if you wish, come and live at Qneitra. I am even willing... to purchase your land. ...Is this sorted now?

I cannot make the fellow understand! What difference does it make to me if I lived here or I lived there, once forced to leave Mansura? The same road leads to Qneitra and to Damascus.

I'm not selling, nor am I about to leave my village. It's clear to me you just don't understand. This land is mine, I am therefore free to sell or to stay on, and as it is, I'm not intending to leave. It's never crossed my mind to give up the smallest parcel, and it doesn't suit me now. And this...this is final.

You forget about the war.

You may have defeated the army, but not the land on which I survive. Your victory does not give you any rights over it at all. It's obvious you don't know what it means to me. On that land, I have buried my wife, my son, five cows and two bulls. The soil of this land is fertile. I know it, inch by inch. And it has grown fertile on account of my labour and my sweat.

He stops a moment to get a grip on himself. He's on the edge of tears.

I will never sell, and I will never leave. I will stay on in Mansura until they've all come back. You can kill me if you like. You can't force me to leave.

But I told you. No one. No one is going to come back!

The Governor is shouting now.

Don't you get the point? Go now, to Damascus. There the Syrian government will make it up to you. Tell them you were thrown out! You don't have to tell them we bought anything from you. What do you say to that?

I say I shall not sell the smallest parcel! You don't seem to realise the importance of my land to me. I shall spend the rest of my life there.

Your presence there is not going to be allowed. Nothing's going to hold up our Kibbutz.

I don't know what this Kibbutz is, but I'm not going to leave.

Don't forget I warned you. Now, well. Good bye!

Idriss understood that the interview was over, and that the Governor was mightily displeased. His expression had hardened and he had lost all his former conviviality.

The old man looks at him, unsettled now and uncertain what to say next. He can't make up his mind whether he is afraid or whether he wishes to explain further, to get through, and make his point, his point about his land. He makes a few meaningless gestures with his hands, and then, seeing that the Governor has lost all interest in him, he walks out of the office.

Know this day and take it into your heart. Aaron shall lean both of his hands forcefully upon the live he-goat's head and confess upon it all the wilful transgressions of the children of Israel, all their rebellions, and all their unintentional sins, and he shall place them on the he-goat's head and send it off to the desert with a timely man. The he-goat shall thus carry upon itself all their sins to a precipitous land, and he shall send off the he-goat into the desert. And Aaron shall enter the Tent of Meeting and remove the linen garments that he had worn when he came into the Holy, and there, he shall store them away. And he shall immerse his flesh in a holy place and don his garments. He shall then go out and sacrifice his burnt offering and the people's burnt offering, and he shall effect atonement for himself and for the people in Israel on the day you are going up to Huddersfield via Leeds to do a reading for Keith Hutson in Halifax. You drank too much lager last night, and you put too much dope in your pipe. You need to be on the 2: 48 train to Leeds, and then change for Huddersfield. But don't go out of the house without eating something first. Sometimes you've gone up the road for milk in the morning and then felt weak at the knees before you make it to Azda. That's when you haven't eaten a thing. Take a swig of "from-the-mother". Boil yourself some eggs. What are you going to read? You should definitely read something from *From Inside*. And maybe you should read some of your most recent poems. What about:

I am too frightened to share this poem.
It should be proclaimed from the rooftops.
It would expose their stuff.

Must it be my job though to bring you the proof?
Shadowy forces are watching.

They are deciding what their response should be
In the light of my sharing it.
However much their stuff weighs heavy on the heart,
It would be reckless to raise my head
Above the parapet.

You should read that maybe, and the Sergei Skripal poem you posted on the Internet. And don't dawdle about getting out of here. You need to be down at King's Cross by at least two o'clock. It'll be great to see Keith again. He's such a good poet. Wrote stuff for Coronation Street, and material for Les Dawson, and for Frankie Howard. Now he writes sonnets celebrating the routines of bygone troupers, variety artists, acts. Keith pretends he's a beginner when it comes to poetry, but he has been a professional for decades. I tell him, for chrissake, Keith, you're a professional. He likes a poem to have a form. Don't we all? Just as a day has a form, a certain day, a certain form, as evidenced by the Hebrew calendar. For instance, this particular day, here in the UK – the 16th of April 2018, in point of fact – is when – if a man has a se'eith, a sappachath, or a bahereth on the skin of his flesh, and it forms a lesion of tzara'ath, he shall be brought to the kohen, or to one of his sons, the kohanim. And though I may not be clear about what this all means, what is clear as day is that the day has a form to it. It's the day when the kohen will look at the lesion on the skin of a man's flesh, and if hair in the lesion has turned white and the appearance of the lesion is deeper than the skin of his flesh, then it is a lesion of tzara'ath. When the kohen sees this, he shall pronounce him unclean. But if it is a white bahereth on the skin of his flesh, and its appearance is not deeper than the skin and its hair has not turned white, the kohen shall quarantine the lesion for seven days. And on the seventh day, the kohen shall see him. And, behold! We could be talking about Herpes, or verrucas or warts – and so the kohen shall quarantine him for seven days a second time. And this goes on and on – on the day I am seized with a seizure on the 2: 48 to Leeds. It happens somewhere in the middle of Cambridgeshire, when our train stops, because the train ahead of us has hit an object. An object on the line. What does this mean in poetry? I am sitting across from a beautiful dark-haired girl, and I am sitting next to a plump red-haired woman. I have bought a bottle of Ribena in the mall at Saint Pancras, the mall which still feels new to me, since I remember how it was when it seemed abandoned. A deserted cathedral. I take sips from my bottle occasionally as we raise our eyebrows and speculate about what the train ahead may have hit. The whole carriage is shaking with repressed electricity. It is shaking violently. I might read for a bit, but I drop my spectacles beneath the table which has my Ribena on it. Christ, this is embarrassing. Apologetically, I ask if the plump woman would mind moving while I get down on my knees and grope around under the table for my spectacles. At last I locate them. We settle back into our places. I might read for a bit, or I might have a little sleep. And now he's supporting me at the same time as he hauls me out of my seat. I am horizontal next; helpless, on a stretcher. The ambulance man's head is very close to mine. I can see trees, an avenue of trees, on either side of the road we are leaving behind. I can see the trees through the double windows of the ambulance's rear door. I am still horizontal. I don't think I did say to him, you're pulling my leg. I think he simply said to me, Listen, mate, I am not pulling your leg. You kept on saying, that's my Ribena.

He joined the Israeli Defence Force as a soldier specialising in education, but later decided that he was meant for the field. His name was Yehuda. In Hebrew the meaning is *Praised*. Yehuda is Judah, the lion. Founder of their tribe, that is, the tribe that took over Southern Palestine: from Jerusalem to the depths of the Negev. Judah goes unmentioned in the ancient song of Deborah. Apparently it was just some rural backwater. Why am I delving so deeply into all this mythology masquerading as history? Nothing needs to be true. It only needs to be reiterated. Multiple meanings must accrue to it. Whatever it is must attract the commentaries of scholars. History encourages a sense of belonging. Genetic research keeps proving to us all that the racial continuity each history purports to offer is bullshit. London was as polyglot and as racially diverse in Roman times as it is today. My uncle Rufus waded the Thames imagining himself to be a Roman soldier, wading the Thames at Westminster, where their ford was paved. And as for Yehuda, where was he?

There is no continuity. Where we were is only where we may have been. Prove to me, when you wake, that you are the you you were when you dropped off to sleep. You can't. The Buddhists go on about the transmigration of souls; that it's alright, if you die, since you can come back as someone else. But say this happens every blessed day? Say that God is a gamer? Say that our existences are just pieces in his game. Ok, so this morning I woke up as Anthony. And I can recall just about everything about being Anthony. Sure, I can. But face it, all that I recall I'm recalling in the present. All that I am is now. God can arrange that easily. I wouldn't be Anthony today, if I couldn't recall how it was to be Anthony yesterday. But nevertheless, there's this break: the continuity has been broken. Yesterday I could have gone to sleep as you. Or as Donald Trump. For the creator, that's as easy to bring about as any transmigration. Yesterday Rebecca could have been Razan. Unless we manage to stay conscious from start to finish, how can we be sure that we have always been who we seem to be? Just dropping off at night is as bad as being struck across the back of the head with a nightstick. Look, one moment I bent forward, in the slips, getting as close to the bat as I could. I watched the bowler at the other end of the pitch run towards the wicket, swing his arm and bowl a subtle googly and the batsman swung and then, then I'm lying on the grass in the shade, somewhere beyond the boundary, bad in my right eye. Bad. The teachers hovering over me. They said it turned me sulky. Cricket balls are hard. But who came to? I mean, yes, I remember squatting there, ready for the catch, I even remember the ball going crack-bang into my socket. But that is what I remember after the event. Say I was never Anthony who got too close in the slips? Say before that I was Robin, who could sprint like a demon. Yes, it's the case, we remember the truly awful breaks, the time the bumble-bee stung and we became so swollen people looked away as mummy drove us down to the Royal Berks. The hospital. We remember the cricket ball. But the thing is, what gets me, is that, it's all remembered in the next interval, I mean, any god, if there is one, could simply have created us an instant ago. Filling each grain of our bodies with granules of remembered time, supposedly familiar spaces, faces. That's the way he has fun. Like when I've come back from a successful gig in Amsterdam. Yes, we have had a triumph at the Mickery, and I'm back in the Old Kent Road, dapper as shit in my pin-striped suit, staying over a Peter's place before heading back to the farm in Hampshire. I saunter out for chips, cross a dark grove of trees to the chip shop on the corner, order lovely fat English chips, saunter back across the grove and bam. I'm on the ground, I guess he's white, not exactly badly-spoken. I must have looked a fair young mark in my pin-stripes. Give me your cash now, all of it. But is it me who reaches feebly into a pocket, drops cash, cards and even the car-keys into his palm, groggy as shit, bruise the size of an ostrich-egg beginning to swell on the back of my neck? Is it me who says to him, Can I keep my chips?

Sodom, struck with blindness. Why? In Ezekiel, God compares Jerusalem to Sodom, saying "Sodom never did what you and your daughters have done. She and her daughters were arrogant, overfed and unconcerned; they did not help the poor and the needy. They were haughty and did detestable things before me." Didn't two angels come to Sodom one evening. And Lot sat in the gate: and seeing them, he rose up to meet them; and he bowed himself with his face toward the ground; and he said, Behold now, my lords, turn in, I pray you, into your servant's house, and tarry all night, and wash your feet, and ye shall rise up early, and go on your ways. And they said, Nay; but we will abide in the street all night. And he pressed upon them greatly; and so they turned in unto him, and entered into his house; and he made them a feast, and did bake unleavened bread, and they did eat. But before they lay down, the men of the city, even the men of Sodom, compassed the house round, both old and young, all the people from every quarter: and they called unto Lot, and said unto him, Where are the beings which came in to thee this night? bring them out unto us, that we may know them. What does this knowing mean? To know a woman is to have intercourse with her. The men of Sodom, old and young, they wanted to know these visitors, these two angels. The rumour must have gone round. That would have been some esoteric sex. But what did Lot do? He, Lot, went out at the door unto them, and shut the door after him, and said, I pray you, brethren, do not do so wickedly. Behold now, I have two daughters which have not known man; let me, I pray you, bring them out unto you, and do ye to them as is good in your eyes: only unto these my guests do nothing; for therefore came they under the shadow of my roof. That was a lie, though, on Lot's part, since these daughters of his were supposed to be married. Perhaps, since they still resided in his house, they were, in reality, only betrothed. I guess it depends how you spin it. And they said, Stand back. And they said again, This fellow came in to live amongst us, and now he will needs be our judge: now will we deal worse with thee, than with them. And they pressed sore upon the man, even Lot, and came near to break down the door. But the men, the two angels, that is, who Lot had invited within, put forth their hand, and pulled Lot into the house to them, and shut to the door. And they smote the men that were at the door of the house with blindness, both small and great: so that they wearied themselves to find the door. Something similar must have happened to me when I had that very first seizure, the one I don't remember at all. Fay says she found me on the bed. There was shit on the kelim, in the study. There must have been an incident. An episode. An event. I must have been conscious enough to have got to my feet, but finding the bathroom, no, that must have been beyond me. I must have wearied myself to find the door. But none of this I recall. So there is a problem about writing about this event. To me, it's all hearsay on Fay's part. I said as much to the specialist, when Fay insisted that I went to see him. I was indeed dismissive about the entire business. When you feel well, it is hard to imagine that you ever were sick. I was sick for weeks after the April seizures. But I couldn't write about them then. You have to be well enough to write about sickness.

So that it should not enter your mind that the heavens and all their host and the earth and all it contains are separate entities in themselves. Alan Watts has made this point succinctly. I got into him after I read a phrase of his which suggested that you really cannot force yourself to relax. I began reading a book of his – *The Book* – after the seizures last April, after one on the train, and then the one a short interval later, as I arrived at the hospital on a stretcher:

> I seem to be a brief light that flashes but once in all the aeons of time – a rare, complicated, and all-too-delicate organism on the fringe of biological evolution, where the wave of life bursts into individual, sparkling, and multicoloured drops that gleam for a moment only to vanish forever. Under such conditioning it seems impossible and even absurd to realise that my self does not reside in the drop alone, but in the whole surge of energy which ranges from the galaxies to the nuclear fields in my body. At this level of existence "I" am immeasurably old; my forms are infinite and their comings and goings are simply the pulses or vibrations of a single and eternal flow of energy.

Did the rails electrocute my brain?

Hit back twice as hard. I remember my Great Uncle Felix, who was Minister of Justice in Israel in the days of Golda Meyer – an office to which he is said to have brought a reputation for intellect and probity – telling me that this was the strategy, or the policy, of the Israel Defence Force, when dealing with any attack by the fellahin. I was ten, I think. Not older. Visiting Israel with my mother. I didn't know what "fellahin" meant. I thought it was a Hebrew word for a terrorist. It turns out it's an Egyptian word meaning peasant or countryman. And now I recall this phrase when I consider the state-of-mind of Rebecca, the IDF sniper, born into an orthodox family in Boston, Mass. She was, purportedly, the person who shot dead Razan al-Najjar, a first response Palestinian nurse, on the first of June at the fence in Gaza. As a writer, it intrigues me to consider what might have motivated the finger that pulled that trigger. In the Jewish calendar, this very day is when the footsteps of the Messiah have begun to walk the earth in preparation for Armageddon and its judgement. Rebecca was the mother of Jacob, who followed his hairy twin Esau into the world by holding onto his leg – pulling it, if you like. Later, Jacob cheated his elder brother out of his birth-right, offering in its stead "a mess of pottage". Spiritually speaking, these twins are in schizo-phrenic opposition to each other - the uncouth, rough twin who is in the right, and the smooth-talking educated twin who is in the wrong but very much favoured by God. A Talmudic reference relevant to the name Rebecca, says that if someone claims you have cheated him but it turns out that in fact he has cheated you, you are then entitled to twice the value of the amount in question. It is this that reminds me of that IDF principle of "hitting back twice as hard". It certainly applies to what they did to me, if they did anything. The title of that poem I wrote about Sergei Skripal is *Semper Occultus.* That's the motto of the British secret service. For publishing that on the internet I ended up in the Acute Assessment Unit.

Leo, one of my great uncles on the Jewish side, seems to have suffered from seizures. Perhaps it runs in the family. The specialist has put me on Keppra. It works differently from most seizure medicines. It joins with a protein that is involved with the release of certain chemicals called neurotransmitters in the brain. The exact way that these actions lead to decreased seizures is not fully known. I suffered from a total loss of energy when I first started taking it. I had appalling nightmares. My walking became unsteady and I was constantly knocking things over. Sometimes I felt like topping myself. You can't go onto the dose needed to ensure you don't get seizures straight away. The dosage has to be built up gradually. Like I say, when I first started taking it, I felt drained of all energy, I felt like Sergei Skripal lying in hospital. I had the shits, constantly. The more I felt like Sergei Skripal, the more I began to think that somehow, on that train, I had come under attack. Ok, you can call this a delusion, so I'm getting the hallucinations they warn against in the list of Keppra's side-effects. But that's not how I read it. As I see it, an attempt has been made to assassinate me.

Qneitra hasn't changed much since last he was there. Though some of the houses were destroyed and others burnt down, the general aspect of the town is still the same.

He hadn't been there since the war. In fact he never truly enjoyed visiting the town ever since the first time he went there and felt over-whelmed by an uncanny sensation. It was not exactly fear, but the town was so big that he felt diminished, or was it perhaps that he felt this way simply because he felt a stranger among its many inhabitants? He did not believe this was the case, since he had often visited other villages where he knew no one, and yet he hadn't experienced this feeling of uncanniness.

He had gone to Qneitra once, on foot, with his wife. All the way there, he'd felt, as he always did, the sensation of being the strong proud man who is followed by his wife, a few feet behind him, trying in vain to match his pace. Now and then he glanced proudly at her out of the corner of his eye.

They had, that day, gone walking through the town streets, and he had noticed that the streets were swarming with peasants; entities as negligible as himself. He realised that both he and his wife were nothing in that huge place.

He knew there were bigger towns. He'd even visited Damascus once. And he had been informed that there were cities in the world compared to which Damascus seemed as small as Mansura. He had tried hard to figure out the size of such cities and ended up hating them and pitying their inhabitants.

Thus, Idriss had spent all his life in his native village, and when any business brought him to Qneitra or Damascus, he'd always finished that business as quickly as he could; and he'd leave without trying to take in either of these larger places, where, more than anywhere, he felt diminished, ignorant and poor.

But today Qneitra is not as it was. It is a bird with a broken wing, as awkward as was his pregnant wife, when she toiled to match her pace to his, through the streets of that town.

There is a strange, and all-pervading silence, despite the great disturbance created by the presence of an occupying force. The noise made by the original townsfolk had had a different resonance. Idriss now realises just how much he liked that former noise.

He has a pressing urge to go through the streets of the town and meet its inhabitants. A number of them, standing across the street, greet him as though they were expecting his arrival, they all talk at the same time, and Idriss feels he had known them all his life :

Why did the Military Governor send for you ?

Tell us what happened!

What did he want from you?

And now Idriss replies with an angry scorn:

That son of a whore, he wanted to buy my cow!

His listeners look at him and at each other. They shake their heads in disbelief, trying not to laugh.

To buy your cow, you say ?

He wants to buy my land as well.

But why?

He wants me to go off to Damascus.

Yes, but we're asking you why he wants to buy? Come off it. You must be joking!

Do I look like I'm joking?

You want us to believe that they want to buy your cow and your property?

That is what he told me.

Did you sell?

Do you think I'm crazy? Does he think I simply won my cow and my land in a lottery? Has he no idea how much they have cost me? Cost me in my sweat and my toil?

So you didn't sell?

Of course I didn't sell. Would you have sold if he had asked you?

Now listen, listen, old man, it is pretty clear they are planning something against you. Something nasty too.

Let them go to the devil! Why should they want to harm me?

This business of them telling you they want to buy your cow and your land. That's not reassuring. There's got to be a purpose to it.

Well, I don't see how, since I didn't sell.

Look, the point is, they have occupied this district by force. It's not as if they paid for it. They threw everyone out. They killed people and burned down their houses without any reason, and, after all this, you find it natural that they offer to buy, offer to buy your land?

I don't know. I'm just telling you what happened.

It isn't that we don't believe you, but still... it's better for you to leave your village. Listen, we all think so. Come and live with us.

What a thought! If I'd wished to leave my village I'd have agreed to sell.

Well, we all think that anyway they'll take your land away, in their own sweet time. They can take whatever, anything they want.

But if they just take everything, then what's going to happen to us?

Don't you realise we lost the war ?

I didn't lose the war!. It was the army who lost it. My property is... my property. What has the war to do with it? To do with my cow and my fields?

That is precisely why they've attacked us. They've always been after our land.

My land?

All the land, and they'll take yours by force!

God damn it! My sons will be back in a jiffy.

They'll not let them come. Only yesterday they shot a man who was trying to sneak back here, into the town, just to collect a few of his things.

He knows he ought to contradict such guff, but now he's over-whelmed by fatigue, having argued first with the Governor, and then with these craven folk. He says with conviction in his voice:

I recognize neither their strength nor their conquest, and now I am going back to Mansura.

Saying this, he walks away, leaving them perplexed.

He now strides down the streets of Qneitra heedless of what's around him, with a feeling of conviction, of superiority, not only over the towns-people, but also over the enemy, whose soldiers occupy the town. He feels so indifferent and carefree that he doesn't even scowl at a tourist who stops to take his photograph.

However, he begins to wonder whether he should have consulted a friend or an acquaintance, someone who would tell him whether he has done the right thing in refusing to sell his cow and the earth he has tilled. But there's no one left to consult. Anyway, what the devil do those people want with his cow and with the earth he owns? They would no doubt slaughter the cow without knowing how gentle she was and how much milk she was capable of giving. Would they plough the land or would they leave it barren, useless? Would they begin by filling the very ditches that have given him so much to do? There's no doubt that he would miss the nut tree, the vineyard and the ears of the corn. Above all, he would miss the land, its soil, its colour, its odour and taste – which he knows better than anyone. Has he not lived with these things ever since he began to crawl?

No one ever understood his dedication to his toil. There has always been someone to tease him about it:

How long are you going to go on wearing yourself out in the way that you do?

Life may come to a stop one day, but the work will carry on.

Damn the work, Idriss. Why not stop and rest?

To this he used to reply:

Damn all idle people. How can you sit there all day long without doing a thing?

Don't you ever tire of it?

Of course I do. But then I always rest a while before going back to work. What else should a man do, after he has rested?

He could never understand how any man could wake up in the morning and not grab his axe and spade and go down into the fields. Such a man would be as abnormal as one who, seeing his wife lying beside him, after a month of separation, would not turn to hug her and to kiss her well.

What a generation of sluggards – to want to be fed without making the slightest effort to feed themselves. No wonder they lost the war!

Driven by a strange force, his steps lead him towards the memorial of the unknown soldier. He stops, and his preoccupations plunge him into *deep thought. In retrospect, he sees himself as this unknown soldier, a brown-skinned, younger man with heavy moustaches and dark, candid eyes looking with hope into the future.*

Only there was no future for you, apart from being brought here – to rest as a symbol forever.

The tomb is bare except for a dry and faded wreath, and Idriss contemplates this, regretting not having brought some flowers or some green leaves. As he leans on the memorial stone, he hears the bugle calling. Its call comes from nowhere and from everywhere, as though the soldier himself were calling, calling to him, from beyond eternity…

Yes, you and I are the only stones which remain embedded in this land after the flood of war has washed away all its produce, all its fertile soil.

I know we are. I have refused to abandon the field, just as you are still here, when thousands around you fled without thought. Say, would you sell your tomb and depart, if somebody suggested it? Not you! We shall remain close together, you and I, and I shall often come to visit you for I too have refused to sell my tomb.

The tears, which Idriss has been suppressing, now overwhelm his eyes, and he cannot help but weep, as he holds the memorial stone in his still considerable grip.

But soon it is time to get back home. Idriss throws a last look at the monument and imagines he hears the bugle again. It is certainly the unknown soldier… weeping. He also feels alone. So now he finds a family in me. The unknown soldier is no more unknown. I shall come to visit him.

Idriss walks on, the sound of the bugle echoing in his ears. He walks slowly, accompanying the echo, as if he were walking in a funeral.

At the approach to the village, he takes in the cornfields, stretch-ing vast and desolate. True, the crop is poor. Foreign weeds have stifled most of the good corn-ears by strangling their roots down in the soil, preventing them from getting any nourishment... I must do something about that, he thinks mechanically. Now he looks at the fields and pictures their owners working there as usual in the late afternoon. He smiles as he passes each one of them, cheerfully waving his hand. The fields are not empty after all. They're full of the sound of working people and the voices of young women happily chanting away their fatigue and rooting out the stubborn weeds in the hope of a better crop this year, as they did last year and as they did the year before.

There lies his own field. Idriss has the impression that the land is beckoning to him. The corn stalks smile as he approaches them, the nut tree seems to lean as if it wanted to whisper in his ear. Even the rock which he had been wrestling with all day long, the day before, looks happy to be there as he approaches it.

Idriss is overcome by a sensation of communion with all that surrounds him. He stumbles in every direction, from the nut tree to vineyard, to the spring and then back to the nut tree. How can one leave all these delights to mere strangers? His cow is still where he left her... She must be thirsty, he thinks. He seizes an empty pail which he fills up at the spring. As the cow drinks, he feels her satisfaction in his own throat. He hugs her neck tenderly as he leads her along towards the house.

Now he feels relieved, almost happy. The sight of his cow and of his land have taken all the worry off his chest. He turns to the cow and tells her almost choking, Just imagine they wanted to buy you, old thing!

Here, in the land of milk and honey, we have instituted the Fourth Reich. We have cleansed the country of its fellahin. It's the Lebanon's fault if they keep them in camps, won't offer them work permits and keep them separated from their own population, not allowing them to integrate with the rest of the community. That is just using their status as refugees as a political tool. And anyway, this land was never promised to them. The grains of our genes are imbued with our faith. And since the time of Moses, this land has been promised to us. "This land was ours before we were the land's." That's in a poem by Robert Frost. I remember my teacher reading it out to us in Boston. And that just goes to show that we are on track. As for the fellahin, the Bedouin, the locals, they're all just temporary obstacles in the river of time. These are our orange groves now; flourishing because of the irrigation we have brought to what was a parched, unfortunate terrain. These apartment buildings are our constructions, and there can never be construction without the destruction of what was there before, for that is just the nature of things. That is how things are. We've offered this backwater Europe and America; technology, progress, civilization. And we're going somewhere, we're going to make Eretz Israel a country of which we can be proud. A country that is religiously pure, racially pure as well. We're on track, and it's just no use you trying to pull us up because, up ahead, "the train has hit an object on the line."

I used to aim for the men, but now I aim for the girls. The girls seem to think they can approach our border-fence with impunity. Their hands raised. Fuck their hands. They're acting as a shield, just to get the sling-shot shits back and away from the fence. This is girl on girl. You fuck with us, we fuck with you. We keep low on the ground. We hone our sights. The guys joke about our bums. They say that we look sexy when we shoot. Camouflaged bottoms. Deborah tells me how her friend Hannah had a corporal fuck her while she aimed. He was lying close beside her, giving her instructions in the softest of voices. That lot, getting out of the truck. Wait. Wait for them to get up close. He loosened her belt as he spoke, ever so soft, then down came her fatigues, and of course, as usual, she was going commando.

Most of us do. It's the thing. Wait till you can smell them, Hannah, he whispered, parting her sweet ripe bum, sniffing her there, then coming back up, whispering close to her ear, just wait for a bit. And let things get real wet. But now, now you concentrate, take that fat one out, hanging round at the back. Mmm, what a slippery girl I've got. And now, ever so softly now, feel for the trigger, he said as he mounted her from behind and slid it in, firing off his round in her as Hannah fired off hers, waking up with a hard-on. Fuck. I am not in Gaza. I'm in London. And it's three o'clock. Three in the morning. Feels as hot as it has all day. I almost fall out of bed, knocking my grandfather's book onto the floor. I think it's the Keppra that's making me stagger. *Go Forth and Serve* by Martin Rosenbluth. An account of Jewish life in Germany in the late nineteenth century, followed by an account of his career as the Zionist, collector of the tithes. Tithes required for the establishment of the National Home for the Jews. My mother kept dalmatians. I think of her dalmatians as I take in the three-dimensional dalmatian I bought on a walk by the canal below the Angel with Hugo Williams. It's propped up next to Lorna's bottom, where, in the life-sized photograph of her in my bedroom, she balances upside-down in a handstand on a book, an open book balanced on her feet, as if she were a lectern. I now take a desultory piss, in the bath-room, fortunately; leaning forwards against the wall behind the toilet bowl. We never had males. What did the breeders call them? Sires. Before one bitch got too old for it, she was mated, and we kept one of her bitch puppies, to take her place as the breeding bitch as she grew old and senile. Lineage passed through the female. One was called Dimity, and the next was called Clemency, and the next was called Continuity. One generation was replicated by the next. Well, not exactly. The spots weren't always in the same place. But isn't one generation supposed to replicate another? When you are a breed, that is. When you epitomise a race. Just as every Jew was supposed to do. It seems like only yesterday that I was Martin Rosenbluth.

Being in the country as of right and not on sufferance. As of right, since Moses led us out of Egypt. As of right, since Babylon. It was the Almighty who made us this promise, this promise of a land of milk and honey. And that is how it is, whoever's cow it may have happened to be, whoever's fucking bee. Yes, but being robbed is never something you can take lying down. Unless you are knocked down first. As when I sauntered out of the chip shop in my natty pin-stripe suit around midnight. Happy as Larry. Pleased as Punch about the tour of Holland, or was it Belgium? The tour my performance company had just completed. Maybe his name was Larry. The tall white guy who came up to me from behind as I crossed the patch of ground between Peter's flat and the Old Kent Road where the trees created shadow from the street lamps. As I came back with my chips, he hit me on the back of the head with a night-stick.

I had this zip-up wind-cheater jacket: it had an elasticated waist. I was wearing it in Jerusalem, when my mother and I went wandering through the souk, led by the Arab boy of my own age who had taken as much of a liking to me as I had taken to him. We stopped at a small shop in the souk that was selling souvenirs and handbags. Mum was very taken by a faun handbag made out of a lizard's skin. My father had brought back a lizard from Australia – where he had been sent aboard the *HMT Dunera* which left Liverpool in 1940 bound for Australia, packed with enemy aliens and Nazi sympathisers and a number of Jews who had emigrated earlier to the United Kingdom; however none of the prisoners, some of whom were survivors of the

Arandora Star, (another transport ship which had been sunk ten days earlier) knew where they were heading. It was to be a dreadful journey lasting 57 days. On the second day of the voyage the ship was hit by a German torpedo, however miraculously it did not explode. A second torpedo was fired which narrowly missed the hull. Onboard, the prisoners, with the exception of the upper-class British Nazi sympathisers, were brutally treated and kept below decks. The inadequate sanitary conditions lead to many contracting dysentery and two people died during the voyage. For two and a half years, my father had been cooped-up as an enemy alien, even though a Jew. He loved animals and kept a zoo in the camp in Hay in the middle of the Australian desert (where they kept German p.o.w.s and Nazi sympathisers concentrated in another compound on the other side of the wire, and next to them, in another compound, Italian, and, next to them, Japanese p.o.w.s). At last the authorities released my father, so that he could get back to Britain where he joined up. As for his lizard, its skin had been framed and was proudly displayed in my mother's bedroom. This may explain why my mother was so fascinated by the handbag. Throughout the souk in Jerusalem, you could buy trains of camels. Carved out of olive-wood, there was always a large camel followed by a smaller camel followed by an even smaller one. The camels were connected by chains. In the shop with the handbags, there was a basket containing broken sets of camels. Single camels, or two camels and not three. I asked the shop-keeper if I could have one of these spare camels. Intent on selling the lizard handbag to my mother, he nodded his head. I stuffed the camel into my zipped-up wind-cheater, and then I saw another that I fancied. Again, I asked the shop-keeper if I could have it. Again, he nodded his head. And as for me, from then on, I kept my head down. It was either Burghfield or Bucklebury Common. I was looking smart for once, in my tweed hacking-jacket and jodhpurs. I had spent the morning brushing Dusty's mane and tail. The treasure hunt had been organised by the Pony Club. I spurred Dusty on. I passed Katie on her palomino. We sped across the common. I needed to find a mushroom, or at least a toadstool. I was galloping under the oaks, my eyes raking the ground.

I guess I was ten years old. Maybe a year or two older. Bam. I got knocked off my pony. Not a good idea to go hunting for mushrooms at full gallop over a common where the oaks have branches that hang down ever so low. And this is what is so strange about concussion. One often has vivid memories of the events that led up to the very moment of impact. And then I think that the memory may be influenced by one's own wondering about what happened. It's now as if I can see that oak. But of course, I couldn't have seen it, since I never saw it coming. After that, there is nothing. Only imaginings. How they must have picked me up, dusted me down, put me back on Dusty. Steeldust was his proper name. None of this I recall. Nor do I recall anything after I drifted off into a snooze on the 12.45 from King's Cross, heading up to Leeds, where I was planning to change onto the Huddersfield train. All I recall is the shuddering of the train as we waited for the line to be cleared of the object on it that had caused the train in front of us to stop. Unless even this is an hallucination. Well, I don't believe it is. But I will say that I feel that there is something sinister about the entire business. Ok, you can say, like Becka does, that I am just too immersed in all my conspiracy theories. I believe it happened because I happened to spill the beans about Skripal, or perhaps about Christopher Steele. I don't care if Becca thinks I am just too small a fry. They engineered that object on the line which caused the train ahead to stop. And they have poisons now that leave no trace. That is what is so suspicious about the Skripal case. Why would the Russians have used a poison that could have been traced to their own laboratories? Come off it. Novichok is a poison that can be bought easily on the black market. I am not at all convinced that it was Novichok anyway. More likely something concocted at Porton Down. Porton Down is expanding to attract private companies. But don't let me drift off the point. There was a bruise on my right hand, the hand nearest the large, jovial redhead. I think Mossad had a hand in all this. Whatever the object was that brought the train ahead to a halt, I am sure they put it there. They wanted my train stopped. They wanted my seizure, whatever it was, to hit me while the train was stationary. They didn't want any forensic enquiry concerning the passengers next to me. They wanted to be sure I was taken off the train before I died.

Can it be tomorrow that I will be Razan? Could it have been yesterday that I was Rebecca? I fall asleep, and I am gone. Who knows who I will be when I awake? We like to think that we are each of us the culmination of some argument. Thesis, antithesis, synthesis. Yesterday modified by today and resulting in tomorrow. But why should this be how it works? All that I recall of what it is that makes myself who I am, I recall in the now. In the grain of consciousness the present is: the grain which is the present. And just as particles switch tracks, perhaps we trade our consciousness for that of someone else. Perhaps it happens every time there's a break. Whether we fall asleep, whether we get knocked out, whether we seem to have ended up dead. There was a pillow to rest on, there was the low branch of an oak, there was a bullet that went through her heart. There was a pinprick on my hand.

One year, we set out on a tour, a tour of the holy land. It wasn't, in point of fact, a Hebrew tour. But Uncle Sol wanted to see as much of the Middle East as he could, so he paid for us all to join this tour led by a Methodist preacher. We took in it all, or most of it. The Lebanon, Jordan and Israel itself. After Israel had taken over the Golan Heights, there was no getting into Syria. We took in Baalbek, and Petra. We drove in a coach past the fenced-in places in which the Lebanese kept the Palestinians. Seething insect life. Uncle Sol said that the Lebanese kept them cooped up for political purposes. So that they were there to stir up a grievance. Palestinians, Lebanese, what was the difference? Uncle Sol couldn't see one. Ok, so they had lost their homes within Israel. But had they not been kept cooped up, they could easily have been integrated into the general Lebanese population. That was the view of Uncle Sol, who said he saw it all from an American point of view. It was no use blaming Israel for their existence, these camps. Their existence was down to the Lebanese. I can remember staring out of the coach window. Swarming, seething life. Uncle Sol had changed his name for a Gentile one. So had my own family. Lots of us did that during the war. World War 2, that is. But this was more than ten years after that, before she had even envisioned becoming Yehuda. When she was still a Boston school-girl; scoffing junk, dumb and fat. Ok, so now I may have moved on, from the first person into the third. But ever since I was a kid, ever since I was taken to that army camp, I have done this. Seen myself at a distance. Seen myself in the third person. Seen myself as slim and not fat. Seen myself not as a girl but as a boy. I call it the game of What If? What if I were an ant? What if I were a boy? What if I were a private called Yehuda. What if I had a penis? That was actually how I got into deciding about my life and where it should take me, after I left the kibbutz. I did what I did because I knew what Yehuda would do. Yes, and if you asked me I would tell you. Yehuda, the yid from Boston, you mean? He joined the Israeli Defence Force as a soldier specialising in education, but later decided that he was meant for the field.

Sitting at the doorstep of his house, Idriss dreamily stares at the setting sun. As it draws closer to the horizon, all the shadows seem to accumulate and then, finally, they merge into each other. The evening breeze becomes fresher every minute, and stars begin to appear in the sky, first the very bright ones, then as the sky becomes darker the smallest appear in their turn. The Milky Way is the last to be seen.

As Idriss dreams on, he feels he needs a smoke and remembers that he has run out of tobacco. Why didn't he take some money with him to Qneitra? He could have bought a pack or two. But many things were left at Abu Hani's in the village. Maybe he could get hold of some tobacco there. He will pay Abu Hani next time he sees him.

Idriss gets up and goes towards the village. He walks cautiously, as though trying not to disturb the sleeping houses. When he arrives at Abu Hani's he finds the door is firmly locked, so he goes around to the back of the shop and tries the window. He looks about him, as though afraid somebody might surprise him, and he feels as guilty as if he were a real thief. Inside, the shop smells musty, having been closed for so long. In the dark, Idriss strikes a match; Abu Hani's lamp is still on the table, so he lights it up and looks around.

Nothing has changed. The shelves there are still as empty as they always were, and the chairs arranged in their circle on the floor of the shop. The place is full of memories, the discussions without end and without aim, the arguments of the young soldiers as they played cards or drank the wine which Abu Hani used to smuggle in for them.

The silence weighs on his mind, yet he hears the respiration of many people in the dark corners of the shop. Nervously, he grabs two dusty packs of tobacco, blows out the lamp and goes back out of the same window, closing it tightly behind him.

He feels calmer as he walks towards his house and gets angry with himself for having felt so nervous. He hides one of the packs under the mattress, opens the other and rolls himself a cigarette. Finding the tobacco crisp and desiccated, he sprinkles it with some water and wraps it in an old piece of cloth. Then he sits back and lights his cigarette; ready, at last, for a satisfying smoke .

Suddenly, through the surrounding silence, Idriss senses movement. He looks at his cow, and sees her calmly flapping her tail. It couldn't have been her that moved, and these are human footsteps.

As he gets to his feet, a young man springs suddenly out of the darkness. He is carrying a rifle, a knapsack and a canteen. His head is wrapped up in a big kerchief showing only his face. Idriss draws himself back: Could he be a thief, or an Israeli? He gets ready to put up a fight, but the young man's eyes reassure him.

Allah be with you. Don't be afraid. I am an Arab.

He unwraps his headgear, and Idriss can see that this is a very young man.

You're welcome, he replies.

They go into the house and Idriss wonders whether he could be one of their soldiers, one of those who lost their way during the retreat. But no, he simply can't be. The war has been over for ten months now.

They sit side by side on the carpet.

Are you living alone? the young man asks.

Yes, and so are you, I see.

Yes, and I hope I'm not disturbing you. I've just arrived in these parts, and as I saw you light up, I thought I might get food off you. You see, I'm dying of hunger.

You're welcome here. My house is your house.

The old man gets up hurriedly and brings some pieces of dry bread from a pan; he sprinkles them with water and places them before the young man.

I must apologize, this is all I have for the moment... but I can prepare some burghul if you can wait a few minutes.

Thank you very much, I can wait.

The old man lights up a fire, fills a saucepan with water and burghul and places this on the fire.

This is Al-Mansura, isn't it?

Yes.

I'm not far from Qneitra then.

The old man puts a few more sticks into the fire under the saucepan, still wondering who this young man could be. Curious, he inquires :

Do you know this region well?

On the map, as I know my hand.

Where are you from?

Jerusalem.

How did you get so far from there?

Yesterday, I lost my way. Couldn't join my mates. Then I worked out that I was already in Syria.

What have you been doing, over where you were?

Fighting.

The young man smiles now, quietly.

You were what?

Fighting.

Fighting whom?

The enemy, of course, the Zionists.

But the war is over, months ago.

Not for us, we're still fighting.

How very strange. I thought all that had ended. Are you a soldier then?

No. I was at University.

And you've left school, in order to fight?

Yes.

Unable to fully comprehend the young man's purpose, Idriss quietly lifts the saucepan off the fire, pours the burghul into a big dish and places it in front of his visitor.

Would you care for an onion?

Yes, thank you very much. Will you eat with me?

I'll have a bite — just to keep you company. I'm sorry I can't offer more.

This is more than enough, really!

As the young man starts eating, greedily, Idriss continues his questions:

I am sorry if I ask too many questions, but… I don't fully grasp what you've told me.

What is it that you don't understand ?

You said you were not a soldier.

I'm not.

And yet, you are fighting?

Well, it's like this. You know what happened in June and how our armies were defeated. But this doesn't mean that the war is over. It's not over, and it's our duty to let the enemy see that he cannot settle permanently in these territories he has simply occupied.

Do you think there's any hope ?

Of course there is, otherwise we wouldn't have gone on fighting.

Idriss looks at the young man: here is another intelligent being—one who refuses to give up.

You know, I've always said, we were not defeated.

We should have started our resistance long ago. We're late in going about it. Not too late to begin though.

Are there lots of you then?

Of course.

A hundred?

Thousands.

Ah, that's good! Idriss warmly asserts, enthusiastic now.

Not good enough. We all must join in the fight.

What about those who don't?

Many do nothing, it's true. But I'm certain they are ashamed of themselves and envy us when we die for our country.

Here is another one abandoned by his neighbours. Idriss looks intently at the young man who is eating still. I haven't offered him much, he reflects. Why not kill the cow? This lad deserves it, heartily deserves it. He should have a hearty meal.

Wait! don't eat any more burghul. I'm going to prepare a better meal.

No, thank you, now I've had enough.

Are you sure?

Anyway, I can't hang around here. We'll talk a little if you like; but first of all, please, understand. Don't breathe a word to anyone about me. You could get into trouble.

I am not a child.

Not even to your closest friends in the village. They could get into trouble as well.

You don't fret about that, Idriss replies with a sigh

Why do you sigh? Are you unwell?

That's to say I can't tell anyone because… I am all alone, in this village.

All alone?

Yes, all alone.

I don't understand. How could you be?

I didn't want to run away.

Why did you stay on?

I'd nowhere to go. Here, I have my land. And anyway, I am waiting for them to come back.

The fighter looks reflectively at Idriss. His white hair, his determined attitude, his eyes moist with suppressed tears. It affects him deeply.

Have they bothered you?

Well, not so much, until today. They took me to Qneitra. At first I was frightened, who wouldn't be? And then I found out. Can you guess?… They wanted… to buy my cow.

Buy your cow?

Yes. That's what the Military Governor told me. They couldn't understand what she means to me. The Governor got angry when I refused to sell! He said they wanted to build something here, a kibosh or a carwash, and that's why they needed the cow. But I told him flatly that I will never sell!

The young man laughed and so did Idriss. The younger laugh rang clear in the silent night. The old man felt happy and relieved to hear that laugh after he had been subjected to the mocking jeers of those Israeli soldiers.

May I ask you for a cigarette?

Yes, for sure, I've got some damp tobacco.

Unwrapping the pack which he had just opened, Idriss hands it over.

Do you want me to roll one for you?

No, thanks. That I can do for myself, says the young man, standing up.

Where are you going? asks the old man.

Morning will be here soon, and I must cross the border while it's dark.

Why don't you take this pack?

No, really, I mustn't.

But upon the old man's insistence, the young man takes the pack and gets a few coins out of his pocket.

Don't do that, chides Idriss. Put that back in your pocket. You should be ashamed!

This'll be for my next visit.

Not a word! Tonight or any night, this house is yours. You will always be welcome.

Thank you so much!

They leave the house and walk a little way together. Then the young man stops and says:

Now I must say good-bye.

Peace be with you.

As the young man walks away, tears begin to roll down the cheeks of the old man. He feels as though he has just parted with his own son, his son, setting out on a dangerous mission.

Son! he shouts.

Yes , what is it? asks the young man, turning around.

You didn't tell me your name.

Do you have to know? You know we only use assumed names. We keep our real names to ourselves.

You're right, I guess. It doesn't matter much.

What do you call your eldest son?

Hamed

Well, then, call me Hamed.

Do you have to go? Why don't you stay on with me? We might bring back life to this village.

No, I'm sorry, but I can't. My duty is to carry on the fight.

You're right. I'd follow you myself if I were not so old.

Your staying here is itself a fight. And it's highly likely that I'll need you in the future. Why the tears, old man?

I am so worried about you.

No need to worry. Have no fear. It will all be right in the end.

I am afraid, Hamed, that something will happen to you.

Death awaits everywhere, but it backs away — that is, if we face it down.

Is there any use though in dying?

Yes, of course there is!

Is there no other way?

No, this is the only way, the only way that's left to save our countries.

Ah, but death is mean, Hamed.

Don't give up. Our God is compassionate.

I've seen them run away, in their thousands.

And soon you'll see them back, returning in their thousands, to run away no more but to fight for liberation.

And when is this going to be?

After we die.

No, Hamed. Don't die.

Idriss gets to feel that he's speaking like a child.

If I should die, there will be more. More and more like me.

Don't forget to tell them to come this way and visit me.

I won't forget.

God bless you, Hamed, and keep you safe. I'm sorry I've delayed you. Take that foot-path and avoid the heights to your right. There is an outpost up there.

Thank you very much. Good bye!

God be with you! God be with you, Hamed.

Idriss turns his back on the youngster as though he were avoiding looking on and seeing him shot dead. The young man's footsteps become fainter as he moves away down the slope and disappears into the night. Idriss turns and looks at the village plunged now into darkness and deep silence. Away at the edge of the horizon, the lights of Damascus twinkle faintly: flicker of some dim, uncertain hope.

Back home, Idriss now feels acutely alone. He senses that he is abandoned, without any companion, without any support. Why am I left alone? Why did they all go away? And this new Hamed. He is far too young to carry such a burden! They should have all been here to help me make his visit more agreeable. But no, they had to run away, cowards that they are. Where did they bury their pride, their boasting and their egging on? Egging on each other, so vehemently in the village square. Their so big words have proved as empty now as bags of wind. How fiercely they were accustomed to quarrel among themselves over some few inches of soil; and look now, how they've abandoned all their land without raising a finger. Where are those young men who boasted of their courage and their confidence? Where are those fine cops who hung their rifles here, while eating their fill? I am led to believe, as our kids used to say, that their precious rifles were loaded with old rags!

Yet I still care for them all, yes, including the cops, I care for them, even for those I had feuds with in the village. I can hate no more. Our quarrels were quite meaningless. One can't live without quarrelling once in a while. I'll make it up with each and all when they at last come back!

True that, while digging trenches, the soldiers ruined the crops. But now Idriss knows that it was worth it. Now he knows that he must do all he can to help them, whenever they come to him – and ask nothing in return!

Why did he wish for his son's return? That was an age ago, in the morning. He doesn't really need him...He must do his duty and so must I. If I were still young I could have moved the rock easily by now, but I will do it by tomorrow anyway. This damned rock has probably rolled from the top of the hill many years ago. And, lazy as we are, we have allowed it to sink deep into the ground, and become as if a rooted part of the land! We should have acted at once, and got rid of it as soon as it rolled down here! Look now, how I have toiled, all day long without success. And it's still there, still there.

He felt he needed somebody to whom he could relate what happened to him that night. The unexpected arrival of that young man had shaken him. It had awakened in him some hope and had actually animated his courage! He will be certain to tell his children about this! They'll no doubt be ashamed to have left him alone in the village and envy him for having been there to assist a fighter in his fight.

Automatically now, he takes the footpath leading to the cemetery, while an obscure anxiety gropes for his heart. He feels acutely alone and deprived, since he has only his cow and the dead for company. In the dark he finds the way to his wife's grave. Feeling weary and wanting to cry he lies down at the side of the grave, stroking the tombstone with the palm of his hand. This is how he caressed his wife's body. Oh, Hamed's father, he senses her sigh, I feel I am waning away... I am no longer so young...

She should have been there tonight, to see that young man on our doorstep. He reminded me of my youth. She would have prepared him an excellent meal and even laden him down with supplies before he started out again.

Were I still that young!

In his mind, he recalls the words his wife so often used - Stop that Idriss, you aren't a young'un anymore. But he never ever stopped: he knew very well how deeply she loved his caresses. Throughout their married life they had both shown each other the same ardour as on their wedding night. As memories swarm back, the tumult of the marriage ceremony sets his ears ringing; the village young folk dancing the dabke, fetching young lasses singing and shouting… She had a robust and well-rounded figure. Lord, she was attractive. As they lay on their wedding bed after the ceremony was over and most of the guests had left, they could still hear the clamour of the young ones singing below. She had shown a slight resistance at first, mixed with shyness and apprehension, but his kindness and consideration had soon subdued all resistance. That night consecrated their union for ever, for Idriss loved his wife as much as he loved his land, and sometimes, though he was loathe to admit it, he loved her more than his land.

I married you, knowing that you had not exactly fallen in love with me. But our life together, your pregnancies, the hopes and expectations of a good harvest, our small quarrels and reconciliations, the hard work on the fields, my having to hide from those cops, the provisions you brought with your caresses to my hiding place - these drew us closer every day. Soon we learned to be used to one another and to love each other very well.

And tonight, in the dark, alone in the cemetery, he can at last admit to himself what his pride has refused to allow him to admit until this moment.

After your death, I felt completely deprived and lost all interest in life. I was hurt that the children gave me so little consolation. It was as though I'd lost part of myself, as though somebody had deprived me of an eye or an arm. I became somehow…mutilated. The children said you had, at last, found peace and rest. Will they say the same when I am dead myself? They may talk of it among themselves while carrying me to the grave. It is strange how weak seem the ties that bind them to us. I think we liked and respected our parents more. They also liked their children more than ours like us. They have taken themselves off and left me here alone. How could they forget me so easily? Besides, they gave up the cow and the land, as if they cared for nothing but escape. I shall not live with them when they come back.

They fancy that I need them, but I am not an invalid. I shall divide the land among them and leave enough for myself to survive on. I don't need them at all. I only needed you! The cow needs you, too. Every time we go to the field, she raises her head and looks in every direction, as though she expected to see you. Two years, she's been waiting for you now.

Idriss feels his face moist with the tears that trickle down his cheeks into his three-months-old beard. But still he feels relieved as though some heavy stone were taken off his chest. He lays his head on her tombstone, and, lulled by the night breeze, soon sinks away into the deepest of slumbers.

Coming back from Baalbek, our coach drove past the camps. All these years later, I am not quite sure which camp we drove past, or whether I ever knew its name. I am pretty sure I didn't. Didn't even know it had a name. Now, that is in the Autumn of 2018, I know that Shatila houses more than 9,842 registered Palestine refugees. Since the trouble started in Syria, it is said that the camp has been swollen with Syrian refugees. As of 2014, the camp's population is estimated to be from 10,000 to 22,000. This is all fitting into approximately one square kilometre. Palestinians can get zero hours contracts to go work on Saudi sky-scrapers. When their work is done, they get sent back to whichever camp they came from. The work is like being let out of jail on probation. In September 1982, between 762 and 3,500 civilians, mostly Palestinians and Lebanese Shiites, were slaughtered in that camp by the Phalange, a militia comprised of Maronite Catholics for the most part. This is the region of the prickly pear. Their leader, Pierre Gemayel, had been the captain of the Lebanese football team and the president of the Lebanese Football federation. The team went to the Olympic Games of 1936 in Berlin, and there Gemayel saw discipline and order. 'I said to myself: "Why can't we do the same in the Lebanon?" So when the team came back, we created a youth movement.' According to Gemayel, when he was in Berlin, Nazism did not have the reputation that it has now. That, at least, is what he told the journalist Robert Fisk. "Nazism? In every system in the world, you can find something good. But Nazism was not Nazism at all. That word came afterwards. In their system, I saw discipline. And we, in the Middle East, we need discipline more than anything else." Discipline, like they have in Israel, and like we ought to have on our railways, here in Britain, instead of cancellations piled on cancellations, signal failures and strikes backed up against strikes. Privatisation has proved an abject failure. Fat cats like Branson leaching cash out of a system that has only really worked when managed by the Welfare State. And where two companies share the same line, you can't use a ticket purchased from one company to ride on a train owned by the other fucking company. Our whole rail system is a mess. The toilets are squalid. On the Southern services you're very unlikely to secure a seat. At least, for once, the 12.45 Express out of Kings Cross, pulls away from the platform on time. At least it does on April 16, 2018. We settle into our pre-booked seats. Rapidly the train picks up speed. Running on lightning, we hurtle across the country.

I think of teeming insect life whenever someone mentions concentration camps. And I think of the ant, and how you can't study the ant without studying its environment. I think of family members who are victimised, and who then, upon maturity, tend to prey on vulnerable members of their family, evolving out of the chrysalis of their victimisation into predatory monsters. Victim today. Monster tomorrow. No one is exempt. No family is exempt. No state is exempt. You expect the police to maintain law and order. But if you wish to flout laws and provoke disorder, you may very well decide on a career in the police. Paedophiles run care homes, because they want to "work with children". Nurses can be bullies. But can we abide this train of thought? Not for long. It's too painful. We so wish to believe that crime doesn't pay. That family life is benign. That it is patriotic to support the state. We long for the calm flow of progress, the continuity of our race, the homeostasis of society. We see the ant foraging among blades of grass that gently bend as the ant goes for a walk so that he may transfer himself easily onto another flexible blade. We set up our deck-chairs and we lower ourselves, and the sun beams down on us as we relax beside the Seine, and sometimes we wave at the tourists passing by on crowded decks who wave at us just as we wave at the chimpanzees in the zoo. And we say to ourselves, you see, life doesn't have to be a mess. It doesn't have to be stressful. You don't have to be herded behind barbed wire. Not all the time. Things can go wrong, for sure, but things can also feel so right. Predictably, the Seine flows towards the sea, just as it will tomorrow afternoon, when you come here again and lower yourself into your deckchair facing the sun. Let that feeling of rightness take you over. Lunch will prompt us to choose a restaurant sometime after breakfast. Penetrative sex leads to babies, crawling leads to toddling, and in your teens your breasts will sprout if you are a girl, your voice will break if you are a boy, and, if you are transitioning, the hormones will kick in, and your skin will seem softer, or your muscles harder, depending on which way you're heading. Winter ends. Spring begins. Day follows night. Breakfast comes before lunch. You wake up each morning, don't you, memory intact?

We just flew over Syria. Gamal Abdel Nasser has vowed to reconquer Palestine. After a five-year disappearance, Burgess and Maclean have resurfaced in the Soviet Union. My first cousin, Jamie, reckons that his father was the "third man". That's on the English side, my mother's side, I mean. Elvis Presley breaks into the charts with *Heartbreak Hotel*. Norma Jean Mortenson turns into Marilyn Monroe. Every day you wake up, you just imagine yourself to be whoever you were before you went to sleep. You're reading *Brave New World* – it's the only English book on your cousin Jonah's kibbutz. It's in paper-back. In less than a week, you'll be eleven years old. If you are you tomorrow. You and Jonah have been joking about this. You are staying with him for a week. Mum isn't with you, for once in your life. Well, there's more to that. She left you before your first birthday, you've been told, to spend a year in Israel. Did she go seeking another Aley? A replacement for the Jew who had died on a motorbike near Naples in the last days of the war. Then she came back and made you her surrogate husband. Then it was that you became inseparable. Jonah's point is that you wake up feeling you are you, because you've got your memories of who you are. But, still, all those memories exist for you today: they're simply part of who you seem to be. Just as the Alpha products of *Brave New World* could be filled with their Alpha conditioning or filled with their Beta conditioning if they were Betas. Here and now, this morning, you pluck an orange off the tree as Anthony, but maybe you were Jonah, before you fell asleep. Maybe he was you. You tell him, that's how it feels to you, after you've had a knock on the head. Like when you were fielding in the slips and got too close to the batsman. And then, the next thing is, you are lying on the grass outside the boundary and the teachers are bending over you anxiously. But that was three years ago. What if you came to as William the Conqueror or Moses? Why should you wake up in the same century as you fell asleep? "Que Sera, Sera. Whatever Will Be, Will Be." Maybe, when you wake up, that won't even have been recorded yet. 45s won't have been invented. Oh, come on, they were invented back in 1949. You can remember that. If you are you, and not Razan.

The River Jordan writhed below us, writhed like a holy snake. We had flown over the Golan Heights. These heights were Syrian territory then. Flowing southward from its sources in the mountainous area where Israel, Syria and the Lebanon meet, the Jordan passes through the Sea of Galilee and ends, polluted, in the Dead Sea. A large part of its 320-kilometre length forms the border between Israel and Jordan in the north and the West Bank and Jordan in the south. The river falls 950 metres from its source to the Dead Sea. For most of its course down the Jordan Rift Valley, it flows well below sea level. Down flows the river Dan, from the Anti-Lebanon mountains and then, at the confluence of the Hasbani, Dan, and Baniyas rivers, it becomes the Jordan. Its waters originate in the snows that cap the 10,000-foot peaks of Mount Hermon. I had an Uncle Hermon. And Mount Hermon is the northernmost point in Israel, and melting snows sink deep into the mountain, forming subterranean water ways which burst out into gushing springs at three major points at the foot of the mountain, and the Banias and Hasbani waterfalls promise such lyric fecundity – irrigating the land of milk and honey. Our land. The promised land. I have her in my sights.

Can I have this one? I now showed the shop-keeper an exceptionally large camel. He raised his eyebrows. Each of these camels was carved out of olive wood. Now the Israelis carve machine-guns out of the trunks of the olive groves they have confiscated from the Palestinians. They give these to their daughters, and to their sons. The shop-keeper was just completing the sale of the lizard bag to my mother. Nodding to me, he continued with the blandishments he was directing at her. She was fairly pretty in a sturdy, curly-haired way, I think. At ten, I couldn't judge, couldn't view my mother from an aesthetic or an erotic point-of-view. My zip-up jacket was now heavily pregnant. A year before she had been chased round and round a lilo by a Greek sailor, while we were on holiday in Corfu. She kept tipping me into the water, to cause a distraction to his ardent pursuit, much to my annoyance. The sale completed, we sauntered out of the shop, but ten yards down the lane of this bazaar, the Arab boy who had befriended me arrested me. Now he called the shop-keeper indignantly. My zip-up jacket suffered a Caesarean. There was no need to cut Rebecca open. Joseph grabbed his brother by his hairy ankle. Esau came out easily. His grasping brother followed him. Joseph, the smooth-talker. Deborah used to make jokes about how hairy I used to be, down below, whenever we showered together. Now I'm as smooth as an L.A porn-star. Deborah says she liked me hairy more. There are these forces in me, I feel. I can be hairy and I can be smooth. Somehow, though, it all gets so mixed up. It's like the sadistic older guy who starts on you all charm, he's just trying to help you with your homework, he just wants you to go out looking neat, that's why he's bought you those cool sneakers, yes, but don't tell mum, she might take it the wrong way. Tell her you won them in a school competition, then you've got this secret that you share, this little lie, and pretty soon he's stroking your hair and saying you look lovely, how you've grown, and would you like some real cool underwear? You don't see where he's going till he's got there. Then there's your grandpa. He just takes you to his shed and fucks you. He doesn't ask to do it. He just knows you're plump and shy. He just pulls apart your legs. He's really kind of kind. He lets you know from the start what he's going to take. He's rough and hard and he rapes you, yes, but at least your fucking feelings don't get so mixed up in it. I've got both these boys in me. Except that they're not boys. But I've got the rough and the smooth. And when I'm smooth I'm mean and cool. That's when I take aim. How was I to know that silly bitch of a shit would set me up? She got what was coming to her alright, but she managed to get what was coming to her all over the fucking media. Now my commanding officer wants me under surveillance at all times.

Camel after camel after camel. They just spilt out of my jacket. Of course, the trader was incensed. There wasn't enough English to explain. Mortified by shame, just as I was when my gran caught me stealing from her bag, I couldn't help feeling guilt as well. Because, after all, I had taken advantage of a misunderstanding. I had known, deep-down of course, that he thought I was simply swapping this camel for that. And worst of all, I would never see my comrade again, who had taken me to meet his mum, in the backstreets of the old city that was then still part of the Kingdom of Jordan. Never get to say goodbye with comradely affection. Now I was a thief. That's how he thought of me. Gathering the camels of his people unto myself. Living with a lion in my bedroom. Flying out of the window of my room in Pearmans Grove, where the puppets that go poking up out of the Velux windows in the roof are still dancing above the attic, as they danced at my wedding in the 60s, gesticulating at Marvin, the American comic who was my best man. I spiral upwards over the roof, upwards above the fir tree I can climb to the top of, the one next to the garage. Looking down now, I can see my revolver in its holster, it's been flung up onto the corrugated garage roof. Why on earth did I not think of looking there? Now all I have to do is float down to the roof and retrieve it. Trouble is I can't seem to get the floating down sorted out. I'm ok with the up. But down just isn't working. Down is just getting smaller and smaller below me, and every attempt at down just takes me up. Since I increased the dosage, I have been having these nightmares.

I am approaching the fence. Or is it her? Is she approaching the fence? In my dream it's me. But on the sites, it's Razan, that bitch, with her hands in the air. I don't know anything about her. I don't want to know anything about her. She was a shield, a human shield. That's what they do, these medics, these aid-workers, these journalists. They get between us and the shits who stone us, spit at us, fire into our settlements. Hit back twice as hard. If there must be victims, so be it. But they're the victims this time. Never again will our Hebrew race be victimised. Moshe Dayan showed the way. Odin had one eye. He knew what we needed to do, turn Zion into Valhalla. Our jeep goes hell-for-leather across the terrain.

The sun is already high when Idriss opens his eyes. The heat has penetrated his light thobe and made him sweat profusely. As he rubs the sleep from his eyes, he wonders how he could have slept so deeply and so long on a tombstone for pillow. As memory gradually comes back, he remembers with a start that he did not give the cow her morning meal.

I have also missed my morning prayer, he says to himself, but without much concern. He has too many things on his mind. The memory of that young man with knapsack and canteen still causes him anxiety.

Shall I ever see him again? Perhaps we didn't have as much in common as I thought. I can't see him going to sleep on a tombstone in a cemetery, mumbling to a grave. He's more an advocate of action.

Angry with himself, he pushes open the door of his house and drags out the cow, not caring to look her in the face.

Hardly has he taken a step towards his field than he stops, struck with shock and awe. A fire is spreading rapidly over all the fields surrounding the village. He hardly trusts his eyes. The flames are everywhere. Desperate, he runs here and there, gesticulating, shouting out:

Fire! Fire!

It doesn't arise in his mind that nobody's there to hear him. He tries to put out the flames closest to him; first by throwing handfuls of earth on them, then by stamping the blazing stalks with his feet. Seeing the paltry effect of his efforts, he pulls off his thobe and tries to beat the fire out with this. But how can he alone confront this conflagration?

One after the other, the fields are devoured. The fire spreads at speed. Hopelessly, Idriss goes on beating the flames with his thobe, inevitably slowing down, but still shouting:

Fire! Fire!

Somebody must hear. Somebody must come to the rescue.

But you're alone, alone, Idriss. You can go on calling until doomsday. Nobody is going to come. Where are those stupid idiots? Why not here, to see their fields burn?

Fire! Fire!

He can't stop himself calling for help, although there is just the sky to hear. His eyes are filled with tears, partly because of the smoke. But utter grief eats at the root of these tears:

Fire! Fire! Fire!

The heat is intense, unbearable both from the sun and from the flames which are inexorably transforming the fields into one huge oven. This land which thrived on care is now being roasted. There is no pity to this scorching of the earth. No, this cannot be! Half-naked, Idriss plunges into the smoke, still beating right and left with his thobe.

What can I do? Oh god, what can I do? A fire so immense, and I am all alone.

All alone, exhausted and dejected, Idriss throws himself down and beats the ground with his hand, sobbing and groaning.

Suddenly he hears footsteps. Animated by a new hope, he raises his head and stands up. Several Israeli soldiers are coming towards him. Clearly, they have heard his cries and are running to help him. They're not so bad after all. He feels he's prepared to be grateful to them for seeing him in trouble, since they haven't hesitated to come to the rescue.

Without saying a word, uplifted by a new fighting spirit, Idriss begins again to beat at the flames with his thobe. Very soon, however, he notes that the soldiers have not made any indication that they are going to help. They stand there unimpressed, their eyes looking vacantly at the devastation.

Idriss stops and looks at them with astonishment. He calls on them to hurry. Then, one of them comes up to him with a hard look on his face and seizes him roughly by the shoulder. Idriss mutters:

The fire! Look, I am trying to put it out.

He looks around at the other soldiers, really appealing for help. No one is moved; not a face exhibits the slightest sign of concern. And now it dawns upon Idriss that they might themselves have set the fields on fire.

The fire here is ruining the harvest, don't you see? Have you no heart? Take these acres, take the produce, yes, but please don't let them burn. True, the harvest isn't as rich this year, but still it has some value. You can still use much of it, to feed the animals, at least.

The soldiers just look on, silent and shut off from him. Never in his life has Idriss felt so much hatred. Out of his mind with rage, he throws himself on the nearest soldier with clenched fists, then on the second soldier. The third is ready with the butt of his rifle – which sends Idriss sprawling, senseless.

Presently, he comes to. His head aches. He feels sick in the stomach. As memory gradually comes back, he remembers all that has happened. Some fields have changed into a huge carpets of cinders and black smouldering charcoal; others in the distance are still burning. Why are they doing this? he wonders, and cannot find an answer. He walks slowly down the hill towards the village. A thickening veil of smoke covers the fields and obscures the view. The land is mourning, now, he says to himself, but they have only burned the crop. The land remains and will remain. The cinders will make it all the more fertile. Be on your guard, my land: Don't give them your crop. Keep everything for the ones who are coming back.

On coming closer to the village he is astonished to hear people talking and making a fair bit of noise. Have they come back, at last? Idriss quickens his pace. There's the first house. People are standing at its door, but they look like soldiers. Idriss realises that they are Israeli soldiers trying to force the door. He lets out his breath in dismay. The soldiers are carrying household effects out of another house, while close by, a military truck is already half-loaded with furniture and other objects taken from various houses in the village.

His anger threatens to overwhelm him as he presses towards the group of soldiers:

You there! Don't you realise these houses have their owners?

The soldiers turn around and look at him. He generates a mixture of surprise and disbelief.

Who the hell is that? inquires one of the them.

They all stop and gather round the half-naked, dishevelled old man who dares to intervene in their business. Heedless of them, Idriss walks towards a young soldier carrying a mattress. He snatches the mattress so energetically that the soldier loses his balance and falls over.

The other soldiers burst out laughing; the mattress carrier joining in as he recovers from his surprise, much to the old man's irritation, as he continues to carry the mattress back into its house. Having done this, he returns to the truck with the purpose of emptying its contents. The soldiers, amused, gather round to tease him.

Do you suppose these houses have no owners? he asks again.

One of the soldiers, simulating great distress, now intervenes:

I'm terribly sorry, is this your house?

No, but it has its owner.

Where's the owner? . . . asks another soldier.

He went away during the war, but he'll be back soon, once things settle down.

With great conviction, he goes on:

Yes, they will all come back. Every one of them. What am I going to tell them when they find their houses empty? And what right have you to take all their belongings?

Then he stops abruptly, as he see by the look in their eyes they're not listening.

Are you alone in this village? inquires the one who seems to be their leader.

Yes.

Good. . .

He goes on in broken Arabic, We shall give you a receipt. When your neighbour comes back you can send him to pick up his belongings. You can if you want do the same for all the other houses, we shall bring you all the receipts tomorrow, is that ok?

The other soldiers look on without understanding what their leader is saying, but when he explains his proposition in their own ugly tongue, they all split their sides. The old man stares at them, perplexed and undecided. He senses that he's said too much already, and his thoughts go back once more to that young man with the kerchief, the canteen and the rifle. Had he been here now, this situation wouldn't be the same. He feels awful, on the edge, but now his pride keeps him from showing any weakness.

It seems you don't believe us, the leader goes on. Well, then, show us your house and we shall be careful not to touch it.

Surrounded by the band of soldiers, Idriss has the feeling of being their prisoner. Other soldiers go on plundering the remaining houses. One of them carries a radio set and dances indecently to a crazy tune.

The leader of the group notices the cow on top of the hill, and he asks Idriss:

Is that your cow?

Yes.

And you pretend to care about your neighbours' property? What if your cow should spoil your neighbour's crop?

Idriss is on the point of answering that there's nothing left to be spoiled since they've already burnt everything. But he keeps silent. He is very tired and now senses the futility of it all.

An officer in a jeep pulls up, and seeing the group of soldiers surrounding Idriss, he reprimands them loudly. They break up their circle and disperse, either to fasten things put on the truck or to enter the houses and go on with their plundering.

The officer looks at Idriss, then pushes him aside. He talks to the leader of the group who now speaks to the old man.

The officer says he doesn't want to see you around anymore. Now beat it!

Humiliated, Idriss keeps his head down and slowly walks towards his cow. His mind is so troubled now that he cannot think of anything. He takes hold of the cow and pulls her after him.

Revolted and boiling with anger, he wants to cry but his eyes remain dry and vacant. Completely exhausted, be leads the cow home silently. His cow walks behind him, quietly contemplating the smouldering fields and the village whose houses are now bare.

Alone with his cow, he sits, as if in deep thought.

The truck pulls out at last, loaded with its loot. Only a few soldiers stay on. The officer seems to be giving them some sort of instructions. Idriss has lost all interest in things around him, and his head falls forward now as though he were falling asleep.

Next, a bullet sings past his ear. Idriss starts and despite his great lassitude he turns towards the soldiers.

Missed, says one of them. Let me try again.

Idriss hears a second shot just as he feels a sharp pain in his neck. He utters a cry, falls on his side. Blood flows quickly from his wound. His last thoughts go to that young man with rifle and kerchief...won't find me, when he comes again. Will they bury me? If there were at least somebody... If...

Blood floods out of the wound, soaking the earth with its darkness. Now a last tremor racks his body and he goes limp, the blood-wet soil clinging to his face that at last finds its repose.

In the quarry there had been carved out a massive rectangular block of stone. It remains the best piece of minimal art I have ever seen.

According to an article by Elif Batuman, writing in the *New Yorker*, the monumental two-thousand-year-old temple to Jupiter at Baalbek sits atop three thousand-ton stone blocks such as this one. The article, which I paraphrase, points out that the pillars of Stonehenge weigh about a fortieth of that. The blocks originated in a nearby limestone quarry, where you can see what archaeologists are calling the largest block from antiquity. Nobody seems to know on whose orders it was cut, or why, or how it came to be abandoned. Baalbek is named for Baal, the Phoenician deity. For the historian, Dell Upton, the site is a metaphor for the role of imaginative distortion in architectural history. In the absence of concrete information, he writes, Baalbek has become "a very accommodating screen upon which to project strikingly varied stories." Local legends maintain that Cain built the temple to hide from the wrath of God; or giants built it, at Nimrod's command, and then it came to be called the Tower of Babel; Solomon built it, with the assistance of djinns, as a stupendous palace for the Queen of Sheba. It is said that the reason some blocks were left in the quarry is that the djinns went on strike. Perhaps they were displaced Palestinians, all on zero-hour contracts. Testimony to Baalbek's flummoxing properties can be found in the 1860 diary of the Scottish traveller David Urquhart, whose mental capacities were "paralyzed" by "the impossibility of any solution." Urquhart is perplexed by the "riddles" posed by these giant stones: "so enormous, as to shut out every other thought, and yet to fill the mind only with trouble." What, for example, was the point of cutting such enormous rocks? And why do it out there in the middle of nowhere, instead of in a capital or port? Why were there no other sites that looked in the least like Baalbek? And why had the work been abandoned midway? Urquhart concludes that the temple must have been built by contemporaries of Noah, using the same technological prowess that enabled the construction of the ark. Work was halted because of the flood, which swept away all the similar sites, leaving the enigma of Baalbek alone on the face of the earth. The purpose of the investigation that turned up the new stone block was precisely to ascertain how the three temple blocks were transported, and why two others like them were left in the quarry. One of these previously discovered megaliths, exposed for centuries, is known as the Hajjar al-Hibla, or the Stone of the Pregnant Woman. That makes me think of my mother, pregnant with me when she hears of the death of my father. This mighty, pregnant stone must have been the one I saw in 1956. It turns out to have a crack in it that would have impeded its transport by a human-driven winch or some gigantic sledge. Perhaps the biggest mystery remains the question of size. Nothing puzzles archaeologists so much as impracticality, and although the karst topography of Baalbek demands strong foundation stones, and although one big stone is easier to move than many smaller stones, the pillars holding up the temple's podium are bigger than they need to be. In fact, Baalbek is one of a series of ancient projects that are under rigorous study by the Germans for being unnecessarily large. Did the podium at Baalbek have to be big enough to serve as an intergalactic landing pad, as documented in the Epic of Gilgamesh? In recent months, archaeological research around the site has been blocked by clashes between Syrian militants, the Lebanese Sunni, and the Shiite Hezbollah. Two weeks ago, in Ras Baalbek, about twenty-five miles north of the temple of Jupiter, six Lebanese soldiers were ambushed and killed by Syrian gunmen. Last Sunday, Syrian refugee tents in the Baalbek region were set on fire. The archaeologists left the site some time ago. The giant stone they unearthed was discovered in June, during a "period of silence" in the fighting, though the team waited until December to make an announcement.

It isn't clear when the dig will resume. It isn't clear when there will be another "period of silence". Not for a while, Rebecca reflected, as she put down the *New Yorker* and lit a cigarette. When it comes, we can all get on with our lives. But that day will only be when we have the region to ourselves. The shits will have to have withered away like the grass. For they shall soon be cut down like the grass, and wither as the green herb. What would she give for a joint? And coach parties from Jerusalem will then set out for Baalbek, full of excited tourists. This will be the outcome. This is what will be. We've always been the ones with the superior technology. Deborah came in, exhausted, all her kit on her back. Fuck, I'm fucking crucified, she said. She had been put on pack-drill for answering back. Answering back when their officer made a dirty remark. Telling him that was uncalled for. Now she threw down her kit, stripped out of her uniform and lay down heavily in her underwear on her bed. She stank. Rebecca mimed a toke. Deborah heaved herself up with a sigh, and went out to the john and, miracle of miracles, she came back with just what Becca craved. She lit up and for once she didn't Bogart the joint. Becca inhaled and held it in. And then she did her a little wriggly dance.

> "We got our IWI ACE Tavors,
> We got our X95s,
> We got our IWI Negevs too,
> We got our Uzis, Jerichos
> And Desert Eagle pistols, you."

She took another drag.

> "We got Galil Galatzis – our semi-automatic
> Sniper rifles, all for you. We got 'em all.

We got 'em all! And you can crap your pants.
Our shooting platform's built by FAB Defense."

Eretz Israel has somehow morphed into Sodom. Or so they say, the
shits who support the shits. They just can't accept that Israel is a
lioness. If to be done with suffering is to cause suffering, so be it. If
the shit-support shits on us, it's because we will never repent. We will
not return to suffering the humiliation of the penalties that repen-
tance will inevitably entail. We will not allow those hairy, uncouth
fellahin back into our versions of Bel-Air. This would entail showing
mercy. But what mercy was shown to us? Weren't we herded onto the
death-trucks? If righteousness entails victimisation, then, yes. Yes, we
turn our backs on such righteousness. Righteousness like that, it's
the meekness of the Goys. Where did meek and mild get the Dachau
lot? Therefore we embrace wickedness. Wickedness is strength. The
Nazis showed us that. It is true that Abraham inquired of the Lord
if he would spare the city if fifty righteous people could be found in
it, to which the Lord agreed he would not destroy it for the sake of
the righteous yet dwelling therein. But let's face it, the meek have
all absconded from Israel. Left it in droves since the start of the mil-
lennium. Just as they quietly departed from Sodom. So of course,
Abraham knew that he was nowhere near the mark. And so Abraham
then inquired of God for mercy at lower numbers (first forty-five,
then forty, then thirty, then twenty, and finally at ten), with the Lord
agreeing, toying for once with the notion of mercy. And it was then
that the two angels were sent to Sodom to ascertain whether these
ten righteous ones could be found. For righteous, read forgiving, or
atheist, or democratic socialist or whatever. And though they were
met by Abraham's nephew Lot, who convinced the angels to lodge
with him, and they ate with him, the crowd that gathered as the

news got round were far from meek and mild. All they wanted was to know the angels. Ok, so they were said to be neither male nor female. Didn't they still have behinds? How could even an angel get by without a behind? What was the stink of an angel's behind? Did they have arseholes at all? Lot who is just a visitor here, he has two of these weirdos staying in his house. Sensational. We want to know. Do these extra-terrestrials have arses? We demand to know. And we have got good at breaking down doors. We have become adept. Basic training sees to that. Breaking down doors and booting you out. You and your angelic fucking shits. And while we may be blind to what you call your fucking rights, don't you believe all that you read in the bible. Why? Because we have you in our sights. Our commanding officer gets us all to watch *Day of the Jackal.*

Sodom, whose people God has made blind. A people who pull the wool over their own eyes. Yes, a people who sit in judgement on others, their heavy woollen wigs grossly interfering with their vision. A people who had set out to set up a democracy, a genuine democracy in the Middle East, at the same time as their own terrorists were assassinating British officers; officers of the armed forces that had taken on Hitler and beaten him. A people who still erect monuments to their own terrorist outfits even as they disavow terrorism and accuse others of being terrorists with whom they will never negotiate. One of their own terrorist outfits was the Lehi – the "Fighters for the Freedom of Israel" – which my mother referred to as the Stern Gang. And she was the one whe told me how my father, a serving British officer in the R.E.M.E., loathed the Stern Gang. Look it up and you are told that this was a Zionist paramilitary organization founded by Avraham ("Yair") Stern in Palestine, while Palestine was under the mandate of the Brits. The aim of the gang was to evict the

British authorities from Palestine by resort to force, allowing Jews unrestricted immigration, as well as the formation of a Jewish state, a "new totalitarian Hebrew republic". The outfit was initially called the National Military Organization in Israel, upon being founded in August 1940, but was renamed Lehi (the Freedom Fighters) a month later. Stern's gang split from the Irgun militant group in 1940 in order to continue fighting the British during World War II. So who were the Irgun? Well, they were another terrorist organisation, of which Menachem Begin was the leader (who later became Prime Minister of Israel in 1977, wresting power away from the Labour Party there). Their right wing, but non-religious policy was based on what was then called Revisionist Zionism founded by one Ze'ev Jabotinsky. "The policy of the new organization was based squarely on Jabotinsky's teachings: every Jew had the right to enter Palestine; only active retaliation would deter the Arabs; only armed force would ensure the Jewish state". Now that I find myself delving into all this, I discover that two of the operations for which the Irgun is best known are the bombing of the King David Hotel in Jerusalem in 1946 and the Deir Yassin massacre of a Palestinian village, carried out together with Lehi in 1948. I've always thought that the Stern Gang bombed the King David Hotel, where British officers resided in the Mandate days, so now it turns out I was wrong, but perhaps not as wrong as all that. Both Irgun and Lehi were vicious, extremist organisations. Back in wartime, Yair Stern initially sought an alliance with Fascist Italy and Nazi Germany, offering to fight alongside them against the British in return for the transfer of all Jews from Nazi-occupied Europe to Palestine. Believing that Nazi Germany was a lesser enemy of the Jews than Britain, Lehi twice attempted to form an alliance with the Nazis. During World War II, it declared that it would establish a Jewish state based upon "nationalist and totalitarian principles".

None of this was familiar to me at the age of ten, when I was proud to be half-Jewish, as I thought of myself, proud to be the nephew of Pinhas Rosen, leader of the Progressive Party in Israel, and Minister of Justice in a coalition born of the proportional representation he promoted as a Liberal. His chauffeur kept a revolver in the glove compartment of his car. I was impressed, as any boy of my age would be. At the time I was partial to revolvers. I stole from my mother's bag in order to go down to the toyshops in Reading and buy revolvers. I had flint-locks too. I had a cache of weaponry, augmented as the amounts I stole got bigger and bigger, since my mother never seemed to be aware of any of my robberies. But this was a real revolver. Not a toy. I liked my uncle's chauffeur. He was someone a boy could admire. He was handsome and strong and he would take me down the street to buy falafel from an Arab vendor who would be dropping his falafels into simmering oil over a stove erected on the pavement. It was he who drove my uncle, my mother and me down to Beersheba. It was he who knew where to find a dune that reared its head high above other dunes in a tract of genuine desert, such as I had always wanted to see. How glorious it was to roll and roll all the way down this dune! I think it was on the way home that I rolled; on the way back to Jerusalem from Beersheba. Beersheba where my uncle had danced among the Bedouin, prompting an Israeli newspaper to publish a cartoon of him dancing the very next day. The Minister dances. Why does he dance?

I stood there on the dais, at the unveiling of the six-branched candlestick with its seventh central stem. My Great Uncle Felix stood beside me. I stood there in my school uniform. I had no idea what all this meant, at the time. As for the menorah, its seven lamps may allude to the branches of human knowledge, represented by the six lamps inclined inwards towards, and symbolically guided by, the light of God, which is represented by its central lamp. The menorah also symbolizes the creation in seven days, with the central light representing the Sabbath. I've noticed also that on an ancient Khakassian petroglyph, perhaps 7000 years old, there's a Menorah-headed man, or shaman, or god; a being with seven heads; so, while it certainly dates back to the time of the tributes to Rome, exacted by Titus, perhaps the Menorah is a symbol adopted by Jewry, or at least shared by very ancient cultures, including the Neolithic ancestors of the Khazars. The Hindu goddess Manasa was depicted with seven cobras behind her head, and the world tree, the Lote-Tree of the utmost boundary that marks the end of the seventh heaven of the Muslims is also depicted with seven branches. But now I come to think of it, how strange it was that my mother had packed my school uniform. Why on earth would I need my uniform on holiday? I realise, in retrospect, that I had been set up. My uniform was needed more than me in the Land of Milk and Honey. I was not standing on that dais because my uncle was proud of me. I was just a puppet. I was not standing on that dais because he was proud of my dead father for having served in the British armed forces against Hitler. He had his hand in my glove, my Uncle Felix. I was standing on that dais as... a token gesture. I was the British Schoolboy. Hadn't the UK government commissioned the menorah from a Jewish sculptor living in London, and then had it shipped to Jerusalem, to be set up in the rose-garden of the Knesset? There is so much I was not aware of, at that time, at the age of ten, and even later, indeed. For instance, until today, as I write this down, I was only vaguely aware that Uncle Felix, a long-term friend of David Ben-Gurion, fell out with him over the Lavon affair. This refers to a botched Israeli sabotage operation in Egypt, in which my Uncle sided with Lavon, when the latter, the

Minister of Defense, who had been (almost certainly falsely) accused of masterminding this disastrous mission, was forced to resign. In meetings with prime minister Moshe Sharett, Lavon denied any knowledge of the operation. When Binyamin Gibli, chief of Israel's military intelligence directorate Aman, contradicted Lavon, Sharett commissioned a board of inquiry that was unable to find conclusive evidence that Lavon *had* authorized the operation. Lavon put the blame squarely on the shoulders of Shimon Peres, secretary general of the Defense Ministry, and he arraigned Gibli for insubordination and criminal negligence. Sharett, however, sided with Peres (who had, along with Moshe Dayan, testified against Lavon), after which Lavon resigned and Ben-Gurion succeeded Lavon as Minister of Defense. Uncle Felix and Ben-Gurion never spoke to each other again. The sabotage operation itself was a particularly shady business, proving to us now that false flags are nothing new. In the summer of 1954, Gibli had initiated 'Operation Susannah'; the goal of which was to carry out bombings and other acts of sabotage in Egypt, with the aim of devising terrorist atrocities there and creating an atmosphere in which the British and American opponents of British withdrawal from Egypt would be able to gain the upper hand and block any withdrawal by generating public insecurity as well as bringing about arrests, demonstrations and acts of revenge, while totally conceal-ing the Israeli factor. Suspicion was intended to fall on the Muslim Brotherhood, on the Communists, 'unspecified malcontents' or 'local nationalists'. The operation was a flop: the cell was betrayed by a double-agent, while suicides, hangings and long terms of imprison-ment in Egyptian jails were the result. Does my Uncle's departure from overseeing Israel's courts of law signal an erosion of their reputation for rigour and probity? As for the multi-fingered candle-stick, I was not all that impressed. As sculptures go, it looked pretty much like…well, a candle-stick. Admittedly, it was large. I preferred my cousin Peter's sculpture. Peter (Yitzhak) Danziger did lovely, modernist, angular sculptures of sheep. He made the controversial sculpture *Nimrod*. I was already sophisticated, as far as sculpture was concerned. I made my sculpture in plasticine. My father had loved making sculptures as a boy. He used to make wonderful horses, very accurately galloping, and fired and glazed to perfection. I made horses in plasticine, and I wanted soon to make them out of clay and have them baked and glazed. I seem to remember that we visited Peter's studio in Tel Aviv. Yitzhak Danziger. In the family tradition, he had one European and one Hebrew name. I guess that goes for me too. I'm Anthony Michael Howell. I think the Michael is meant to be pronounced *Mic-haël*, as it would be in Hebrew. It is only now, at seventy-three, as I research this text that you're reading, that I've realised all this. An angelic name (my God, the irony!): Anthony – "who is like God" – Howell. Howell, though, not Rosenbluth. Howell, because my father took my mother's Gentile name, during the war, for had he been captured he would have been in deep trouble had his name been Rosenbluth. Had he been discovered as a Rosen-bluth by the Nazis or by the fascists, he would have been victimised, sent, in all probability, to a concentration camp instead of to a camp for prisoners-of-war. However, my father was no victim. He was a warrior. He was fighting back. His name should not have been Eli, after the high priest who cared for Samuel as a child. And even that was changed when he joined the forces, changed into Aley, as if he were as Welsh as the name "Howell" suggested. How deceptive we are, whoever we may be. Standing in front of his motor-bike with its lethal side-car, looking grim and dangerous, my father, who was killed on that motor-bike, should have been re-named something far more militant. Judah, for instance, who Jacob – himself re-named as Israel – chose as his champion, his warrior son. Judah is a lion's whelp: from the prey, my son, you are gone up. He stooped down, he crouchéd as a lion, and, as a lioness, who shall rouse him up?

Later, we visited Syria, seeking out kelims. Our house in Kentish Town had a bedroom arranged like a Moorish parlour: three sides for reclining, arranged around an eight-legged coffee table, where intense discussions about art and poetry would take place, accompanied by a fair amount of marijuana intake and the occasional orgy. This was the sixties. There were kelims everywhere. In those days, some of us headed off for India, in the "magic bus", some of us headed for New York. Signe and I loved exploring the Middle East. We travelled around Turkey, Iran and Syria. The souk in Aleppo was one of our favourite places. Baskets of exotic grains, stacks of kelims and carpets, decorated robes and thobes on display, bargains struck over little cups of coffee, seething crowds, with only the tourists in contemporary dress. Wandering there, we think we saw John Cleese, being a tourist himself, head and shoulders above the crowds. That was where the funny walks must have come from, being so tall, trying to look smaller, Signe my wife did that too. She was tall, even for a Norwegian. Trying to look smaller than you were. Wandering through the souk was like wandering through another century, and this jolted my memory, recalling how it felt to wander through the old city of Jerusalem before it became part of Israel. And now so many of these ancient places have been destroyed, either through the bombs of war or through the depredations of the construction industry. Israel demolishes the ancient villages of the Druze and the Bedouin. But is it so different to anywhere else in the world? Tottenham, for instance. Where White Hart Lane Stadium rises inexorably upwards like the Tower of Babel. Not to mention the "Manhattanisation" of

Tottenham Hale. The West Indian community centre was demolished seven years ago, and now a multi-story block of luxury flats is going up there. We've lost our recycled furniture store: the council refused to fund it any more. And we now have to get into a car and travel several miles to get to any form of rubbish dump or recycling plant. The one by the corner of the park was closed down last year so that the site could be used by the academy school they intend to build next to it, the same academy which has just had all its pupils' exam results annulled for giving them extra help in exams. Israel's recent history is that of the up-to-date Western world, intent on gentrification. Haringey's answer to poverty is to get rid of it by getting rid of the poor, booting them out of the borough. Israel does the same. It just does it with a mite more savagery. Mind you, here in Tottenham, knife crime is on the up. All that this means is, here it's all arranged far more subtly. Get the poor to stab themselves to death. You don't need to exterminate them deliberately. Let 'em do it to themselves. That's why we have got rid of all the youth clubs and community centres. Many modern poisons leave no trace. No trace of the past, that is. I look across at Shiva, standing on one leg, in a dancing pose, on my small revolving bookcase. In one of his many hands, he holds the drum of creation, in another, the flame of destruction. Shiva should be the patron deity of developers. For all construction involves destruction. We cut down the olive groves, not to diss the Palestinians, just to make room for luxury villas with stainless blue swimming-pools. Each London tower-block is haunted by what had been built on the site before it was constructed, just as that which had been built before was haunted by what was there before it was built. Thus Israel will always be haunted by Palestine. Whether a trace of it remains or not. Whether they manage to silence their critics or not, as they've tried to silence me, travelling up to

Huddersfield to do my poetry reading for Keith Hutson in Halifax. And you may decry what I'm saying, as Becca does so mockingly. But there was something fishy about what happened to me on that train. The train ahead arrested by an obstacle. The whole carriage shaking with suppressed, confounded, arrested electricity, and me being far too scared to share my poem. Ok, you retort, ok, Anthony, but where is the evidence? Why should there be evidence? Many modern poisons leave no trace.

It was just too heavy to lift. That great, rectangular block. Or maybe it had cracked. Yes, the one I saw when I was there did have a massive crack in it. I can remember that, because one end was still embedded in the earth, and you could get up onto it and walk up its incline, thirty, forty feet off the ground. But since then, their excavations have gone deeper, and recently they've managed to unearth another, intact, but equally massive: one just as immovable block. I met a traveller from an antique land, and what were the words, there, writ on the pedestal? There, where the lone and level sands stretched away into the distance? "My name is Ozymandias, King of Kings. Look on my Works, ye Mighty, and despair!" That was in Junior High. We were studying Shelley. There was that romantic guy, that English teacher from England. Anthony. David said he let him suck his cock. A block as immovable as a trauma. A trauma that began in some army camp perhaps. That army camp. What happened there? And here I am in another. In another army camp. Back then, there was that unslim, passive girl, dressed in that neat but overtight little outfit. Uncle Sol had given it her in secret. Neat little dress that clung to the hips, and the coolest fashion-label sneakers. Mind you, they were already plump, those hips. Plump enough to get ragged about in school. But wasn't she the princess in that army camp? Was it at Hanscom,

Ipswich or the navel yard? Military bases. And nice bungalows for
the armed services to swap their wives in, and later, later, at college,
laughing students would tell me about the parties that had gone on,
over at Hanscom and Ipswich – and in the yard. And I would let
them joke about those goings one, without exactly sharing in the
joke. Keeping kind of quiet, like that plump, passive girl had kept
about the dress and the sneakers. They were her secret, weren't they,
only shared with Uncle Sol? Why am I dwelling on this? It was all so
many years ago. In some other lifetime. I should face the reality of
where I am now. Confined to barracks for obeying orders, fuck it, for
obeying fucking orders. When you're in the army and you kill, that's
not murder. That is just doing your duty. That's been done with the
legal team there to back you up. Simple as that. So why does the press
want to get at me? Get to me, rather? Get at and get to Rebecca, me,
Yehuda. Me. Get to that fat girl. Maybe I was her yesterday.

He gave me this book he had written, *The Old Man and the Land*.
His name was Mamdouh Adwan. Having taken us to Craq des Che-
valiers and some of the other wonderful places in Syria, it was his
parting gift to me, as we said goodbye in Damascus. I cherished this
gift from a fellow poet, but I never bothered to read it. There is your
Western arrogance for you. I was put off by the title. Back in 1971 or
'2 (the book was first published in Damascus in '71) I considered the
title a rip-off of Hemingway's *The Old Man and the Sea*. And because
it didn't strike me as terribly original to adapt a Hemingway title, I
never opened the book. Turning the title page over now, I see that
the Arabic title of this work is actually translated as *The Mutilated*. I
think I would call it *Mutilation*. It's translated by Loy Ajjan, in a way
that feels faithful to the original, but is quite often incorrect, so far as
its English goes. On the back-cover, it says that Mamdouh's novelette

was inspired by one of the events he experienced after the aggression of June 1967, when Israel annexed the Golan Heights. The frontispiece has a quote from Mahmud Darwish:

If you wish to grasp the sun first sink deep into the earth my friend.
Thus does the tree by its roots when reaching for the clouds with
fragrant flowers and tasty fruit.

In the original it says, first sink deep into the *land*. But earth seems more appropriate. So the title could also have been, *The Old Man and the Earth,* which seems more accurate. In the spirit of this psychoanalysis of state and soul, I have decided to annex this novelette, and print *Mutilation* here, within the pages of *Consciousness.* Annexation, after all, is what has happened to the Golan Heights. And the fact of the matter is, we do need them annexed. People never seem to realise that the Golan overlooks more or less the whole of Israel. We can't allow the enemy to set up its batteries on these heights. They are a direct threat to us. The heights overlook Galilee and Tiberius and the Jordan valley. They are like the ramparts of a castle. You can't just hand a castle back to the enemy. Back in Boston, there wasn't an enemy. Not exactly. Uncle Sol was nice to me. Too nice perhaps. He got me those sneakers. Cool, so far as it goes. He was definitely no way near as direct as Opa, who just began touching me up when I was fat, knowing I wouldn't resist. In a sort of way, though, Opa was more, well, benign. At least he made no attempt to seduce me. I knew he was just going to be filthy with me. Just a filthy old shit who was going to get his boner into his granddaughter. Uncle Sol was a sadist though, taking us on this holiday and that, buying me those sneakers, then the neat little dress, building up our secrets. Uncle Sol was not content to penis me and get it over with. He was a fucking brute to me, because he made me fall in love with him. I cared for Uncle Sol. And he made sure I did, so that I would never ever tell. And that was fine, until I was a girl no more, right at the end of my teens. Somehow my turning into a woman seemed to turn him off. I no longer had much appeal for him. That was when he started on my sister. That was when I wanted to kill her. That was when I realised what a shit he was, and went all mental and Orthodox. After that he had me packed off to that kibbutz. Back in Boston, I was becoming, well, a loose cannon. The truth is, I resented it at first. Practically being despatched out there, sent like some convict to Israel. But then, when the oranges came to puberty on the bough, when I worked the land, when I first milked that cow, I began to feel that I was actually in the right place for me. Boston was what? A dead sea. I was an Israeli. I was going to make myself as tough as a prickly pear. There was no way I was going to hold on to any residue of that puppy fat. I was going to be a hound. More than a hound. A lioness. And that, well, that I have achieved. And now I am here to avenge the six million abused. I am Judah's lioness. I have been commended for my marksmanship.

There's a blaze of light from the sun above and behind this leaf. From the other side, the leaves look heavily green and opaque. But from underneath, as I look up at this leaf that shades my eyes while I sit in the chair at breakfast time, soaking in the D, I can see just how the light comes wading through granules of space, as the leaf lifts in the breeze, and fields of forceful energy flow between me and the sun. I've been trying to learn what space is recently. Not emptiness. It's not emptiness that surrounds me as I sit beneath the fig in my Tottenham garden, looking up at the sun through this leaf as I turn brown. Ok, from further away, from its other side, the leaf is one green space or shape. From underneath it's a filigree of tributaries, a very complex delta flowing backwards on itself, flooded with, feeding on the light, while draining moisture out of the soil servicing the roots below. My eyesight wades its way through units of time, or rather the sight of the leaf comes wading towards my retina; connecting me with every single thing, though nothing is single. Everything's attached to the elsewhere. So one is many, just as the wave is a particle as well as a wave. Emptiness is therefore metaphysical. A sort of generalisation, illusory. Maybe, maybe it is, but…how lovely it can be, the pause, the rest at the end of some intricate passage. Emptiness our illusory bliss, as expressed by Barnett Newman perhaps, or Morandi. Now I breathe in deep, let out a sigh. It's the seizures that have got me thinking this way. They've made me feel that my fabric through time was just being torn apart – since before these happened to me, I felt I was all of a piece, the past tense being fine to employ about myself. Now I am not so sure. Am I who I was? It is ever so easy to use the past tense about oneself, but memory is something one can only recall in the now, as I've forgotten just how many times I may have already told you now. And since everyone has memories, one could have been anyone yesterday. As of now, or rather, as of when you are reading this, I have been led to believe that I have been Anthony Howell, that I have been him for some considerable time. A lifetime perhaps. Anthony Howell himself remains pretty clear about this, and he would say, of the incidents that occurred on the sixteenth of April 2018, well, he would say, I got up and made myself tea. I grilled myself some cheese on toast. I was feeling a trifle run-down. Too much beer and too much dope. If it's in the house, I can't stop myself. But that morning I had to say to myself, take care. Make sure you make yourself a decent breakfast. I had already packed the night before. I was going up to Huddersfield, to do a poetry reading.

"Anthony, you've been saying that for the last half hour." "Bibi came by at three for his afternoon session. At four he refused to leave and claimed my house was actually his. Then he locked me in the basement overnight while he lavishly entertained his friends upstairs. When I tried to escape, he called me a terrorist and put me in shackles. I begged for mercy, but he said he could hardly grant it to someone who didn't even exist." However, I do exist, I am sure of it, even in my dreams, and on one occasion, I realise that I've managed to get a job as a bus driver, but I interrupt the route I'm on to watch a Sonya Henie movie. It's dark when the movie finishes with her skating on oil-covered ice that reflects the pristine underneath of her tutu. A tramp walks slowly in front of the traffic, allowing me to cross the intersection and get to my bus which is full of passengers who may or may not have paid. I've left the engine running. It's dark, but I take a stab at the controls and getting started. I am driving from the top of the bus. I am not that much in control, and I haven't the faintest clue about the route. I don't seem to stop at the bus-stops – and wouldn't know how to anyway. I am taking my passengers somewhere. But where? To Toulon, perhaps, where the first massacres directly related to the Black Death took place in April 1348. Hygiene rituals, and their relative isolation in a quarter, ensured that the Jews were less affected by the plague than their Christian neighbours. Of course this looked suspicious to the Christians and as a result the Jewish quarter was sacked, and forty Jews were murdered in their homes, and then the same thing happened in Barcelona. In 1349, massacres and persecution spread across Europe, including the Erfurt massacre (1349), the Basel massacre, and massacres in Aragon, and Flanders. 2000 Jews were burnt alive on 14 February 1349 in the "Valentine's Day" Strasbourg massacre, where the plague had not yet affected the city. While the ashes smouldered, Christian residents of Strasbourg sifted through and collected the valuable possessions not consumed by the flames. Of course, this couldn't happen here, not to the Muslims in Bradford, and not here, where I'm in the dark, jumping hedges or fences on a horse, but neither the horse nor I can see what it is we are jumping. It's all guesswork. As it is with the lion. Will he eat me or not? This is what I intend to tell the director as he asks me what I thought of *Phedre*. I stare into my cappuccino. I have been invited to watch the first night. It is pretty clear that this is what you would call an avant-garde production. The text is not utilised or referred to at all. I have however decided to brush up my French. A brown member of the cast approaches me in the bar afterwards. She has smooth brown arms. I try to say to her, in French, may I suck you off? I don't know the verb "to suck". It will feel very nice, I say in English, giving up on the French. Very smooth. I'm missing my front teeth. For this is how things are. Life is not a river.

Life is a collage. The universe an accident. Great Aunt Elsa, wife of the Minister, spent the last years of her life creating dark collages. Broken buildings, streets jammed with rubble, emaciated faces, smoke, shadows.

> And though we yearn for Andromeda, when we learn
> That she's four million light years from our galaxy
> While we are less than a mole on Orion's arm,
> We see once more that we are merely part of things –
> As far from the outer rim of our milk-filled churn
> As we are from that galactic bulge at its core.

Meanwhile, in 1967, my cousin Vera tells me that my boyhood comrade Rafi was twenty-three and a tank-commander in the 6 Day

War. I think it was then that I was wrapping blankets and supplies as a British volunteer, sending humanitarian aid to Israel. As we sent off the last batch from somewhere in Hampstead, one of the men organising the effort winked at me and told me there were machine-guns wrapped up and well-hidden in our blankets. The stories were of a small country, an underdog such as we all knew and loved, battling against impossible odds by launching a surprise attack, of a plucky new nation confronting the combined forces of the Arab world, of brave pilots flying in to bomb Egyptian airfields and missile-sites beyond their range, and then coasting home, using their spent planes as gliders. When I contact him about this text, Rafi writes to me: Dear Anthony, I have fond memories of you in Israel, and in your house in England and also when I came to see you in the Royal ballet, I believe it was 1966, after I finished compulsory army duty. Liz and I had such a good time with you in London, but all the literature you gave us was destroyed in a hurricane (Sandy) with lots of other stuff...As for my army days as a combat officer, in the 6 Day War, I was responsible for 30 people and we all managed to live beyond the war with no deaths, but in the '73 war I was responsible for 100 people, and there were a lot of deaths in our combat unit and a lot is not anything close to WW11, but, in contrast to the 6 Day War, it was devastating. I finished my army as an operational officer responsible for 200 people and ended the army as a major with combat experience, helping the top command of the area of Southern Israel. This does not change how I wake up in the morning, I feel every morning that I am lucky and have the privilege of dealing with all the nonsense of modern life and the conveniences that we have in the western world. And I deeply appreciate it all. I have just had open heart surgery in February... you might laugh to know my aortic valve is pig skin! When we get together in London, you can ask me whatever you want about the army, as I would not know where to begin as I spent 6 years trying to protect the terrible country of Israel… as a soldier and an officer. As the two of us know, life is temporary and the more we think, well, I guess it makes it more interesting! If you can put your thoughts in writing it will be so thought-provoking for me, especially as I cannot express myself in this genre very well." Today Rafi lives with his wife in Brooklyn. Vera says that he is does not consider himself Jewish anymore. He chooses to be an American, just as my father chose to be British. Sometime in the 80s, he and Liz passed through Britain, on their way to Brooklyn, and he said that they saw no future to living in Israel.

> Jaguar swallowed the moon… With a pair of bellows,
> Or with pursed lips, the gusts of March blow things awry….
> The clouds race away, and for once there's a clear night sky.
> Somewhere above, the Archer aims at the sea-goat,
> His arrow that of time. Here and there a satellite
> May be spied on its voyage across this ocean of ink.
> Look for a triangle of dim stars – this is the upper part
> Of the scales that connect the two asymmetrical balances
> That sail across the waters of existence with decks twinkling –
> Like on some liner where a gambler with infinite capital
> And infinite time on his hands is making one of an
> Infinite number of wagers. Scorpios hangs close to the horizon.
> Orion limps across the dark. Aries looks nothing like a ram.
> One familiar ladle swings around the northern pole.
> And the great square of Pegasus gives us a line on Arcturus.

Meanwhile Yehuda is serving in the IDF. He feels good about it to mask feeling bad about it. Last month, his friend David hung himself. It's best to feel good about it. Think oranges. Yehuda was born in Brooklyn. At eighteen he left everything behind to fulfil his dream of living in Israel.

"Who knows?" said the jolly red-haired lady next to me. Could she have done this to me? There is that pinprick between two of the fingers of my right hand. A shadow underneath it. I recall intending to doze off, resting my head against the window of the stationary yet still vibrating carriage. I can't recall the dozing off itself. That's not how it works. But it is after that that she could have done it to me, easily. And of course, I have no recollection. I had already conked out. I have had fantasies that they have been observing me for some time. Working in twelve-hour shifts, perhaps. On salaries far exceeding my own. Because I'm a loose cannon. Because I have spilt the beans about the PNAC. Dual nationality passports. Things like that. Listen. How can you continue to be a neglected poet, how can you persist in writing in a void, without being in possession of the most colossal ego? Whatever Becca says about my not exactly being important enough to come to the attention of Mossad or the deep state or whoever it is the red-haired lady answers to, I, myself, consider myself a threat. I try very hard to stick out like a sore thumb. After all, this justifies my neglect. I use poetry as a form of encapsulation. And my verse keeps up a rustling such as the reeds would create, whispering to each other, after Midas's barber had whispered his secret into that hole by the river's bank. King Midas has asses' ears. Because my poetry is ignored, I can say what I like: dark thoughts, dirty thoughts, subversive ones, perverted ones. Firing off in all directions. And that's why they wanted to get rid of me. A drop on a needle's tip. Or perhaps she scratched me with her nail, and the nail had her poison painted on it in some clandestine nail-bar…Quick as thought, up the demon climbed, and reached the massive outer door of the eagles' nest; and he shook it, and shook it, but he could not get in, for Surya Bai had bolted it. Then he said, 'Let me in, my child, let me in; I'm the Great Eagle, and I have come from very far, and brought you many beautiful jewels; and here is a splendid diamond ring to fit your little finger.' But Surya Bai did not hear him. She was fast asleep. Now the demon tried to force open the door again, but still it was too strong for him. In his efforts, however, he broke off one of his finger-nails – (now the nail of a Rakshas-demon is *the* most poisonous of things) – and this he left sticking in the crack of the door when he went away, empty handed. And the next morning Surya Bai opened all the doors in order to look down on the world below; but when she came to the seventh door a sharp thing, which was sticking in it, ran into her hand, and just like that she fell down dead. At that same moment the two old eagles returned from their twelvemonth's journey, bringing with them a beautiful diamond ring, which they had purloined for their little favourite from the Red Sea, far away. There she lay on the threshold of the nest, beautiful as ever, but dead. The eagles who had raised her as their own offspring could not bear the sight; so they placed the ring on her finger, and then, with loud cries, they flew off, never to return. A while after, there chanced to come by a great Rajah, who was out on a Royal Hunt. He came with hawks, and hounds, and attendants, elephants and horses, and he pitched his camp under the tree in which the eagles' nest was built. Then, when he happened to look up, he saw, amongst the topmost branches, what appeared like a queer sort of tree-house, made of wood and metal, and he got some of his attendants to climb up to see what it was. They soon returned, and told the Rajah that up in the tree was a curious thing like a cage, having seven iron doors, and that on the threshold of the first door lay a fair maiden, richly dressed; that she was dead, and that beside her stood a little cat. At this the Rajah commanded that they should be fetched down, and when he saw Surya Bai he felt very sad to think that she was dead. And he took her hand to feel if it were already stiff; but all her limbs were supple, nor had she become cold as the dead are cold; and, looking again at her hand, the Rajah saw that a sharp thing, like a long thorn, had run into the tender palm, almost far enough to pierce through to the back of her hand. Immediately, he pulled it out, and no sooner had he done so than Surya Bai opened her eyes, and stood up, crying, Where am I? And who are you? Is it a dream, or true? Can things happen to you that you simply have no recollection of, that you just can't remember?

I was feeling jaunty in my snarky pin-stripe suit. We had come to a shuddering stop, although the train had not ceased to shudder, to quiver. My horse went hell-for-leather across the common. I bent forward, in the slips, getting as close to the bat as I could. These memories are crystal-clear. Each is a memory of the moment before I was knocked unconscious or experienced a seizure. And then, I came to, on the ground, his hand pressing my chest, pinning me down, as he demanded my cash. And then I remember being able to see out through the rear windows of the ambulance. And then, I came to on a horse, riding forward, into the night, no idea where I was. And then, I was somewhere beyond the boundary, anxious faces leaning over me. In each case there's a memory of what it was like to come to. And then, after the event, a recollection of what had happened before the event. But in each case, of course, that recollection is occurring in a subsequent present. And therefore it partakes of that present, not of what was prior to the event. Just as Surya-Bei, the lady of the sun, emerges out of the ripened mango, so you re-emerge, re-form, slowly becoming intact once more. But can she be sure she was Surya-Bei, the Surya-Bei that she was before the jealous Ranee drowned her in the tank, before she was changed into a sun-flower that was then pulled up by its roots, and burnt, and its ashes scattered deep in the jungle, where in the spot where the ashes fell, a mango tree grew up straight and tall, and where, from the blossom of this tree, a mango emerged and ripened, and it was she? Can she be sure, before these intervals, that she was not an eaglet, or a jealous Ranee, or a raksha-demon? We can only assume the continuity we experience at breakfast. Much to God's amusement perhaps. When you got up from the sofa, and put your clothes back on, were you the plump, teased schoolgirl you were before your grandpa entered you? Or after your uncle left you to sleep, the sneakers neatly arranged, their heels poking out, just under the bed, after you drifted off, were you the same naïve young teen you were before he began to kiss you? Things happen to you that you can tell no one about, and you wrap them up in cellophane wrapped in masking-tape and then hidden in tin foil and locked away in a box. Then you close your eyes and will the box to shrink and shrink, until it turns to nothingness. And that's that, or so you think. But these big moments that you've shrunk until they've disappeared, they haven't gone, they're under your skin, they have simply dissolved… into your being. Like the time you fell off that ladder in the library, just as Mrs Shackston was about to steady you by putting her fat fingers up your thighs. Like the times your sister showed off her new sneakers and you wanted to kill her. Not only then, there were other times you could have seen her burn in hell, like when she went up to Uni and went all intellectual on her social science course, saying things like, excessive love of clothes betrays a loathing for your body, Becca, (that's when you were still so overweight), or, avowal of a faith shows a disbelief in self (that's after Miriam stole Richard off you and you went back to synagogue), or, don't you know, defence of sect-identity signals individual uncertainty? – (that's when you'd gone all orthodox and kosher). She never let a chance go by to get at you. And then, worst of all, she said, endorsement of any sort of racial purity is just evidence of personal uncleanliness. And you asked her what she meant, and she said, you know what I mean. That was just before Uncle Sol packed you off to the kibbutz. You know what I mean. You know what I mean. She was as unclean as you though, wasn't she? Back before Uni at least, with those sneakers and that dress that she got out of him as well. That was when you thought seriously about turning him in. Uncle Sol. That was when everything was so unclean. That was when Boston was Sodom. Like the times your uncle took you both along to those parties at the army camp.

It was after I had written this poem that the episode occurred. I shouldn't have mentioned Christopher Steele. If there ever was an agent of the deep state, this is he. He's a secret agent who seems remarkably indiscrete. An agent who concocts his intelligence, devising as dodgy a dossier as any published prior to the Second Gulf War. This, though, is his own dossier, which has assiduously painted a damning picture of collusion between Trump and Russia, suggesting that his campaign readily accepted a regular flow of intelligence from the Kremlin, particularly on his Democratic and other political rivals. It also alleges that Russian officials had been "cultivating" Trump as an asset for five years, and had obtained leverage over him, in part by recording videos of him while he engaged in compromising sexual acts, including consorting with Moscow prostitutes who, at his request, urinated on a bed. Trump's supporters threatened legal proceedings. "Legal experts soon assured Steele that the criminal referral was merely a political stunt. Nevertheless, it marked a tense new phase in the investigation into Trump's alleged ties to Russia. The initial bipartisan support in Congress for a serious inquiry into foreign meddling in America's democracy had given way to a partisan brawl", or that is how the far from impartial *New Yorker* expresses it, and goes on to say, "Trump's defenders argued that Steele was not a whistle-blower but a villain – a dishonest Clinton apparatchik who had collaborated with American intelligence and law-enforcement officials to fabricate false charges against Trump and his associates, in a *dastardly* attempt to nullify the 2016 election. According to this version, it was not the President who needed to be investigated but the investigators themselves, starting with Steele. 'They're trying to take down the whole intelligence community!' Steele exclaimed to friends. 'And they're using me as the battering ram to do it.' Steele is considered an expert on Russia, principally because he has never ceased to present material aimed at vilifying Putin and his administration – Putin, who, unlike Yeltsin in Bill Clinton's day, puts his country's interests first and doesn't do Washington's bidding in return for campaign pay-cheques. Since this smearing of Putin serves the interests of the John McCain, Dick Cheney crowd, the duel-passported supporters of the PNAC and the neo-con crooks on the ultra-right, Steele has remained a "valued" authority, having served as a senior officer under John Scarlett, Chief of MI6, from 2004 to 2009. Note that Steele was selected as case officer for Alexander Litvinenko and participated in the investigation of the Litvinenko poisoning in 2006. Naturally it was Steele who "quickly realised that Litvinenko's death 'was a Russian state *hit*'. He likes to advertise himself as being on a hit list of the Russian Security Service, probably with less justification than my own assertion about my own assassination. Sergei Skripal turns out to have been Christopher Steele's associate.

Today he's a trained fighter in IDF intelligence, defending the home he knows and loves. Best of all though, he has managed to get seen by a consultant and asked various questions about his general health as well as being given a physical examination included several measurements of his chest. Consent was of course required for the clinical photography, involving before and after surgery pictures, in order to complete his accurate visual record. Prior hormone treatment was then administered for a period of 18 months. This increased the amount of breast tissue available, and Yehuda was strongly advised to stop smoking, due to increased risk of capsular contracture (a tight, fibrous capsule that forms around an implant). Then details of surgical options were discussed regarding the most appropriate method and the range of implants available. It was explained to him that augmentation surgery could not provide totally natural boobies, so it was important to have realistic expectations and not pre-conceived ideas of perfection regarding the final appearance. Then came the toughest part of the assignment: opening up his scrotum, removing the testicles, and removing the head of the penis to create a clitoris. The shaft and the scrotum were then used to create the labia and vaginal canal that would allow Yehuda to have a perfectly healthy and fulfilled sex life. Basically his penis was flipped inside-out. The head of the penis, still attached to the nerves, was threaded through a newly-made hole in the penis skin to make this clitoris. The urethra was then pulled through the other hole, and the entire inverted penis was pulled into the body to create the vagina, and luckily inverting the penis resulted in a deep enough vagina to fulfil the expectations of his commanding officer. What was left of the scrotum was used to form the outer lips of the vagina, and to add some finishing touches to reduce scarring. And thus an attractive cosmetic result was achieved that corresponded with Yehuda's aesthetic expectations, as well as giving his interior sexual arena sufficient neovaginal depth and neo-clitoral sensation to achieve orgasm. Now Yehuda feels that his body had been something of a theatre of war, but nevertheless the struggle has been worth it. He has been born again, as a girl called Rebecca.

Maybe tomorrow I will wake up as my father, or as my Uncle Paul. It seems to me that we can only perceive continuity from the outside. We see it in the endless cycles of violent assault followed by vengeance followed by violent assault. Most unfortunately, the injured party comes of age to assume the role first taken by the one who injured them, while the one who injured them may well have moved on, into defeat, death or senility. The vengeance is then meted out, not on the perpetrator of the injury but on the one who now occupies the role first taken by the injured party. This is well expressed on the first page of *The Water Babies,* when Charles Kingsley introduces us to Tom the chimney-sweep*:* "He cried half his time, and laughed the other half. He cried when he had to climb the dark flues, rubbing his poor knees and elbows raw; and when the soot got into his eyes, which it did every day in the week; and when his master beat him, which he did every day in the week; and when he had not enough to eat, which happened every day in the week likewise. And he laughed the other half of the day, when he was tossing halfpennies with the other boys, or playing leapfrog over the posts, or bowling stones at the horses' legs as they trotted by, which last was excellent fun, when there was a wall at hand behind which to hide. As for chimney-sweeping, and being hungry, and being beaten, he took all that for the way of the world, like the rain and snow and thunder, and stood manfully with his back to it till it was over, as his old donkey did to a hailstorm; and then shook his ears and was as jolly as ever; and thought of the fine times coming when he would be a man, and a master sweep, and sit in the public-house with a quart of beer and a long pipe, and play cards for silver money, and wear velveteens and ankle-jacks, and keep a white bull dog with one grey ear, and carry her puppies in his pocket, just like a man. And he would have apprentices, one, two, three, if he could. How he would bully them, and knock them about, just as his master did to him; and make them carry home the soot sacks, while he rode before them on his donkey, with a pipe in his mouth and a flower in his buttonhole, like a king at the head of his army. Yes, there were good times coming; and, when his master let him have a pull at the leavings of his beer, Tom was the jolliest boy in the whole town." That is the way of the world, as Tom knows too well. That is the way with families, as with nations. In due course, the oppressed becomes the oppressor. All other notions of continuity are myths. Nothing endures, except these cycles of violence. There are too many skeletons in the cupboard for racial continuity to be assured. The Jews themselves have exaggerated their own caricature, since it serves the myth that their genes are as Judaic as their religion. It is not at all the case. My own Jewish father was blond and blue-eyed, and was invited to join the Hitler Youth in Berlin when he was a boy. Where genetic strains are protected, insulated from genes external to the family, we get hybrid vigour. Perhaps to ensure their dome-skulled, Neanderthal ancestry, the pharaohs were joined in marriage with their sisters. Weakness and incipient, inherited disease was the result, and with each dynasty, the inbred nature of their intercourse led into the tunnel of extinction. Even our personal con-tinuity is far from assured. However much they may deliberately fail to recall it, most men have dreamt not so much of castration as of being possessed of a vagina rather than a penis. However much they may fail to recall it, most women have dreamt not so much of envy as of being in full possession of a penis, rather than a vagina. Perhaps we inherit the dreams of our parents. The dreams of both sexes, whatever our sex may appear to be in some present we acknowledge as our own. Do we go to sleep as the person we were after we woke up? Do we wake up as the person we were before we went to sleep? Sometimes we end up pursuing a dream through reality. Sometimes reality impinges on our dream. Consider how T.E. Lawrence promoted that dream of Arab liberation during the First World War, and stuck to it after hostilities ceased, despite the fact that we had made the Balfour Declaration in 1917 (and addressed it to Lord Rothschild) in order to get American Jews to pressure America to take part in the war, in which we Brits were at a stalemate. Even before that, The Sykes–Picot Agreement, officially known as the Asia Minor Agreement, had, in 1916, created a compact between the United Kingdom and France, to which the Russian Empire assented. This agreement defined their mutually agreed spheres of influence and control in Southwestern Asia, and it was based on the premise that their Triple Entente would succeed in defeating the Ottoman Empire. With the war over, it was time to divide the spoils. Lawrence, who envisioned an independent post-war Arabian state, had sought the right man to lead the Hashemite forces and achieve victory. That man was Faisal, King first of Greater Syria and later of Iraq. Faisal fostered unity between Sunni and Shiite Muslims to encourage common loyalty and promote pan-Arabism with the goal of creating an Arab state that would include Iraq, Syria and the rest of the Fertile Crescent. While in power, Faisal tried to diversify his administration by including different ethnic and religious groups. Lawrence, and the Arab leaders who had fought with him, attended the Paris Peace Conference in 1919, expecting to enjoy the fruits of the sacrifices of their desperate war in the desert and their feats against the Turks.

Instead, Feisal discovered his name had been omitted from the official list of the delegates. In meetings and in speeches he made his presence felt. "The Arabs have long enough suffered under foreign domination," Feisal proclaimed, resplendent in robes of silk and gold. "The hour has at last struck when we are to come into our own again." President Wilson, meeting this Arab leader, said, "Listening to the emir, I think to hear the voice of liberty." Of course, France, Great Britain, the United States, and Italy dominated the negotiations. The French, who had suffered grievously in the war, wanted to punish Germany and the Ottoman and Austro-Hungarian empires. The British acquiesced in this. All three empires disappeared, and soon the conquerors had sown the seeds of modern discontent. Feisal's claims were brushed aside. The French and the British resented Wilsonian idealism about the end of imperialism. "I have returned," gloated Lloyd George, after signing the Treaty of Versailles, "with a pocket full of sovereigns in the shape of the German Colonies." At the San Remo Conference in 1920, France and Britain sliced up the Middle East, creating a collage of their own wishful thought, and drawing sometimes ruler-straight borders, disregarding ethnic, linguistic, and religious affiliations as they conjured up new countries. They called these states "mandates" instead of colonies, but that was what they really were, or were intended to be. Physically, this was cutting a long story short, and like I say, there is no continuity, for few Arabs were satisfied with these divisions, and it appeared that the war would continue in the Middle East, which neither Britain nor France could afford. The cheapest way for the British to wash their hands of this business was a Hashemite solution rewarding Feisal and Abdullah of Jordan with kingdoms fabricated from lines drawn on an empty map. Churchill and his staff renamed Mesopotamia as Iraq, apparently based on what Arab tribes called this region, derived from

Uruk, the name of some ancient Sumerian city. Ignoring the orderly Ottoman system's divisions, they crammed Christian, Jewish, Muslim, Arab, and Kurdish groups into Iraq's artificial borders. Moreover, its tip was snipped off, and made into Kuwait, while Feisal's tribe, the tribe most willing to work with the British, found itself elevated, into royalty. The British then rigged the Iraqi "elections" and Feisal was proclaimed king. Another kingdom was created called Transjordan, which of course outraged the Zionists, who believed this land had been promised *them* by the Balfour Declaration. Regarding Palestine, Feisal and Lawrence made carefully worded statements about its future. Privately, they were convinced that there would be "chronic unrest, and sooner or later civil war in Palestine." Lawrence went into depression. He judged "Our government in Iraq worse than the old Turkish system." This was the system which had beaten him, and, as is so often the pattern, given him a taste for being beaten. Had Tom the sweep survived, perhaps he would have continued with being beaten as well as administering beatings to his apprentices. Lawrence spent the rest of his life trying to escape the heroic monster that he had himself created in the press to achieve his political aims. The beatings he chose to endure were administered by others to exorcise the evil of his tale, he wrote, before dying, like my father, on a motor-bike. In military terms, the Arab Revolt was a harbinger of modern warfare, particularly in the Middle East: operations combining air, land, and sea forces; fast-moving armour supported by mobile troops; and targeted strikes focusing not just on destroying the enemy but also on immobilizing him by severing communication and supply lines, often utilizing powerful improvised explosives. War in the desert, like war at sea, takes place over a vast, often inhospitable landscape, where flanks can be turned indefinitely. Intelligence and agility are essential. Furthermore, in modern warfare as in the revolt, leaders must have military and political skills. Perhaps most important, as successive invaders have learned, while it is relatively easy to enter Middle Eastern countries, tribes and other groups will rise up and fight smart and hard until the enemy withdraws, licking his bloody wounds. Thus, it is of paramount importance to win over the tribes, for they hold the keys to ultimate victory. As we can see today, Britain's and France's conflicting promises and the supercilious fabrication of "states" have created mistrust and cynicism throughout the region. For modern would-be state builders, the aftermath of the Arab Revolt clearly illustrates the impossibility of outsiders attempting to create or even "fix" these inorganic states. As long as such artificial, colonial-created borders remain, there will be instability in the Middle East, according to O'Brien Brown, parts of whose 2010 article *Creating Chaos* (in *The Quarterly Journal of Military History*) have been paraphrased here. O'Brien Brown concludes: "That legacy bodes ill for global security concerns as radicalized leaders—secular or religious, governmental or terrorist—seek ways to right historical wrongs. Indeed, the struggle has already set the stage for conflict in the 21st century, and poses one of the greatest security challenges of our time. Saddam Hussein's 1990 invasion of Kuwait, as monstrous as it was, did have historical grounds. More chilling, Osama bin Laden specifically blamed the Sykes-Picot Agreement for breaking "the Islamic world into fragments." Seek you the ways to 'right historical wrongs' or seek you vengeance in cycles which we can see perpetuating themselves since Biblical time, in which the anger falls, not upon the culprit, but upon whoever best fulfils the role of victim? After 9/11, this was Iraq; for the Zionists now, it's the Palestinians. And yet, we need to take into account our own revolt; our own revolt at these shenanigans. Never should we dismiss the role of compassion, our sense of injustice, the reason-led impulse towards fair play. This prompts me to side with David against Goliath, when reviewing in my mind images from incidents at the fence in Gaza. I see amputees in makeshift wheel-chairs spinning their slings before releasing them to strike at the IDF on the Philistine Israeli side. I see explosions, reduced on the screen to puffs of smoke; mere fireworks to the viewer safely ensconced in his Tottenham home. I see ambulances lurching off, packed with the wounded, or coming back empty to pick up more of the injured, and there is a nurse with her hands in the air, approaching the fence.

One night, a nation went to sleep as a democracy, and the next morning it woke as a fascist regime. This can happen to a country. It can happen to a family. My own mongrel background makes me a sort of democracy that I sometimes find difficult to govern. Half-Jewish, on the wrong side, that is, my father's side – which prevents me from being a Jew according to the Law which is the lore that Judaism is; in other words, according to its own folklore, except that there is no folk, only a religion called Judaism, which my grandfather hoped would be superseded by Zionism. Not at all the hope of my socialist father. Then I'm half-English; my grandfather on that British side being a brigadier, and the youngest general in the British army. He died at the Second Somme, while his wife – who was Granna to me – was an artist descended from a line of Norfolk Quakers. Granna lived in Alma Terrace, in Allen Street, off High Street Kensington, and once, when I was little more than a toddler, we walked to the Cavalry Memorial, when it still occupied its Stanhope Gate position, on Park Lane, before being moved further into the park, after the widening of Park Lane. Underneath Saint George there was a ceremony going on, and, I think, in front of us, a march-past – which I witnessed. After the wreath-laying was over I was taken to shake hands with a very old gentleman who Granna introduced as General Gough. General Sir Hubert de la Poer Gough GCB, GCMG, KCVO, was a senior officer in the British Army in the First World War. A favourite of Field Marshal Sir Douglas Haig, as was my grandfather, he experienced a meteoric rise through the ranks during the war and commanded the British Fifth Army from 1916 to 1918. During the Curragh, before the First World War, both he and my grandfather served in Ireland, but with great misgivings. Many British officers had relatives in Ireland and found it hard to remain impartial "keepers of the peace" (or, at least, keepers of the state-of-affairs) – my grandmother got into the habit of hiding an IRA man in the cupboard while an empire-advocating cousin called in for a cup of tea. There was little sympathy in the army for colonisation. That was old hat. In Africa later, my uncle Paul identified with the Nuer, the fellaheen of the Sudan, if you like. Lawrence inspired the Arabs. My aunt Jean studied the Dinka. Uncle Paul and my father agreed that Israel appeared to be the last spasm of the colonial impulse. But the screen of the Cavalry Memorial is inscribed with the names of imperial cavalry regiments and great leaders, and steeped in colonial history. Just as I stood later with my Jewish uncle at the consecration of the Menorah, I stood with General Gough and my Granna at the march-past. In a sense I epitomise the mixture that epitomises being British. Families encapsulate the tensions of their nations. I admire the tragedies of the ancient Greeks, for they manage to fuse the dynamics of state politics with the throes of family disasters. The egotism of Pentheus brings about the destruction of his palace. Or consider Jocasta; queen consort of Laius, King of Thebes. Laius received an oracle from Delphi which told him that he must not have a child with his wife, or the child would kill him and marry her, while in another version of her story, recorded by Aeschylus, Laius is warned that he can only save his city if he dies childless. But one night, Laius becomes drunk and fathers Oedipus on Jocasta. As the tragedy unfolds, witnessed by the chorus of Thebans, through whose eyes we see the play, the dilemma of the family becomes the dilemma of the state. By fathering Oedipus, Laius becomes complicit in his own downfall. And by marrying Oedipus later, Jocasta becomes complicit in his destruction and hers, which is not only the destruction of their house but also a metaphor for the downfall of their city. My mongrel characteristics I accept as quintessentially Brit. Indeed, I'm very glad that I'm a mongrel; but a mongrel identity is something of a puzzle, and I think it has led me to puzzle things out. I tend to think hard about words, especially when they seem to be presenting me with a puzzle. At present I have been trying to resolve the difference between *compromise* and *complicity*. When I think about compromise, I think of Tony Blair, and the ambitions of career politicians; willing to debase the currency of the viewpoint they represent in order to achieve power. Compromise might sound like a good way to resolve irreconcilable differences, but it proves a slippery slope: a few years later you are a welcome house-guest of a gangster called Berlusconi and intimate buddies with a neo-con president of America. Trouble is, all your life you have compromised, in order to further your own interests. You compromised when you agreed to participate in those Dolphin Square parties, where you were known affectionately as Miranda. All in the merry old Whig tradition. And somewhere down the line, these illicit goings on can be used against you, and you can be blackmailed into endorsing whatever your deep state acquaintances require. While you protect your reputation and your family, you bring about the destruction of a sovereign state. Aeschylus would have told the story well. On the other hand, when I think about complicity, I think about the night-porter and his "little girl" – and how their story is that of Romeo and Juliet, but set against the murkiest backdrop of the twentieth century, a concentration camp. In an essay for the Institute of Psychoanalysis, that I gave recently, I compared the work of Freud to that of Gide, and about how Freud reneged on his own theory of seduction, when considering the abuse of children, shamed into doing so by the Viennese establishment, of which he and his wife were a part. Rather than actually being abused, children were prone to fantasies about their fathers and mothers. However, as I pointed out:

> As for the rejection of the seduction theory, today the pendulum seems to have swung back. Shame acknowledged requires blame. We prefer to credit children with innocence, and to lay the blame on some elder. Statutory rape makes this explicit. What we cannot allow is any hint of complicity.

So society seems to regard compromise as invidious but necessary, while complicity is bad. It's simply not to be entertained. *The Night Porter* came in for a veritable barrage of hostile criticism. But actuality is riddled with complicity. *Fury* cannot avoid encapsulating its own love-story. And take the case of Yehuda, who completed his national service in Israel, in order to be eligible for university. After coming out of the army, he started his BA. He was reading Human Biology, and became fascinated by genetics. It was there that he met a Palestinian girl who shared his enthusiasm for the subject. Her name was Razan. She had lovely smooth brown arms, and sometimes, in the classroom, they shared a desk, and his elbow and her elbow would almost come into contact. When she did her national service she had enlisted in the medical corps. Sometimes Yehuda would lie awake at night, thinking about their elbows, his elbow and hers, and how very nearly they had touched. He wondered if Razan was lying awake in her bedroom thinking about their elbows. They went for coffees together, and they went for falafels together, and they visited the Tel Aviv Museum of Art together where she was amused by Itzhak Danziger's *Sheep of the Negev*. 'They look like desert sheep,' she said, 'so angular – all bones.' She felt that Palestinian artists were under-represented in the collection, and she said it made her feel angry. A month or so later she dropped out of university, and he never saw her again. They had never actually done anything about the elbows. Several years later, he found himself defending the Gaza fence. He was working behind the lines, assisting munitions, sorting clips for the snipers. When the unrest had first started, they had been ordered to supply the snipers with rubber bullets. Later as the situation became more and more hysterical – this is the way he thought of it – they were ordered to send out lethal bullets instead. Yehuda said later that he felt uncomfortable about this. After all, it was no more than hysteria. The Palestinians were never a serious threat. There was no munitions store behind their lines. Then on the tenth of June there was an almighty fuss in the press. Not so much in *Haretz* as in the international press you could google on your laptop when off-duty. A Palestinian nurse had been shot by a sniper as she approached the fence with her hands in the air. He learnt later that her name was Razan.

Perhaps they were practising their assassination technique on me. I should have asked the red-haired woman's name. But why should I have done? She was only a fellow passenger. All I needed to say to her was, excuse me, as I prepared to get down on my hands and knees and scrabble for my spectacles, which had fallen so inconveniently under the carriage table. Becca saw my recent post and said she hardly thought Mossad would consider me important enough to assassinate. But say I had asked her name, the jolly red-haired assassin, and say she had replied. Would she have said her name was Becca, or Rebecca? Becca learnt all this in school. Becca made a comment on my post. She told Becca what her grandparents had told her parents. Becca had no wish to be an accomplice after this fact. It was perfectly possible for Becca to apply for citizenship of her own country. You I get along with, normally I don't, Becca told her once. Becca, look, you gotta toughen up. And you may decry what I'm saying, of course, as Becca does so mockingly. Whatever Becca says about my not exactly being important enough to come to the attention of Mossad or the deep state or whoever it is the red-haired lady answers to, I, myself, consider myself a threat. I am convinced I'm a threat, just as Christopher Steele considers himself a threat to Russia, I told Becca, in a Face Book message to her. Very blond, very intelligent, and very much a socialist, Becca and I had met on a dating site. Katie was also a blond, I recall. Not a blond with straight hair, as was Becca's, but a blond with a head of curly hair that was hard to cram inside a riding-cap. Meanwhile Becca took another drag on Deborah's joint. Deborah was Moshe. Becca was Yehuda. Becca felt so fab as Yehuda in her uniform.

I used to come up to Leeds to visit her – on the same express. Very blond, very intelligent, and very much a socialist, Becca and I had met on a dating site. We went on a holiday once, to the Algarve. We had hired a car, and once we drove deep into the mountains, then parked the car and walked up a track that led us up and up and round the edge of a precipice, and then we found ourselves standing at the foot of crags and we looked up, and we saw eagles circling and spiralling up on the thermals, high above the crags themselves. I enjoyed that holiday, but something about it hadn't worked for her, and she broke things off with me, soon after our return to the UK. I'm not that good with blonds. Perhaps because my mother had dark, curly hair. I have never stayed with a yellow-haired girl for that long, or they have never stayed with me, and when I was a boy, Katie was my riding companion, and a good friend, but not someone to whom I felt particularly attracted. She was a blond with fuzzy hair. She was the girl who was with me when I got swept off my pony by that oak-tree. The hunt was on for mushrooms.

Now I feel so guilty about the sword. One week, the cleaner rang to say that she couldn't come, and that her sister was going to come instead. I agreed to that. Then the sister turned up with her boyfriend. He expressed an interest in the sword. The sister was pretty and they were both chatty and I was so busy looking at the sister that I hardly noticed what the guy was saying. My memory is hazy now about all this. Maybe I was stoned. Maybe he asked if he could borrow the sword for a theatrical production. Maybe I agreed. The sword, the Sandhurst sword-of-honour which had been awarded to my grandfather on his passing out, had been given to me by my Uncle Paul, the uncle on my mother's side; her brother – known by his daughters as the Lämmergeier, on account of his stern look and fierce manner – as if he lived on a steady diet of bones and dyed his feathers red with the blood of lambs. I found him intimidating when, at four years old, I looked up at him. Still, we did have this in common: both of our fathers had died in uniform while we were still in our mothers' wombs. He showed me no affection but gave me a grudging acknowledgement expressed in gifts that were supposed to be treasured: the Hobbs bat, the sword. For years, that stood in its scabbard, leaning against a bookshelf in my study. I hardly noticed it. And then, a week or so after her boyfriend had remarked upon the sword, the cleaner's sister contacted me to say that she also was unable to continue coming to hoover and clean up kitchen and bathroom. Several weeks after that, I glanced in the direction of the sword and noticed it was no longer there. I searched high and low. It was gone. Now I blame myself for this loss. I seemed to have forgotten all about the cleaner cancelling and her sister coming in as her substitute and arriving with a boyfriend in tow. A year or so later, I plucked up the courage to ring the original cleaner and accuse her of stealing my grandfather's sword. This she angrily denied. I now realise that it was not her, but her sister, or rather the boyfriend of her sister who had, in all probability, gone off with the sword. A fine sabre with a decorated hilt in a fine scabbard. I feel as guilty as if I had stolen it myself. Ashamed of my neglect. Ashamed that I hadn't noticed that the sword was missing on the day that it disappeared. I feel guilty about the paintings by Arnesby Brown that got stolen from my mother's farm. Mum was already beginning to suffer from dementia. The farm she had moved into, to be nearer me and Gwendy and our son George, was too big for her at that stage. She boasted to the cleaners about her prized possessions. The door of the farm was never locked. The large Arnesby Brown went first – the one of the cows grazing on a hazy afternoon – very similar to his famous painting of the same cows looking towards the moon, a little later on, in the twilight. But that's a painting in Worcester City Museum called *Herald of the Night*. The thieves knew exactly what to take. However, they left the smaller painting of the windmill in a storm. Adrian, who helped my mother with her horses, a person I intensely disliked as I thought he was manipulating my mother, told me to take the windmill painting. He was sure the thieves would be soon be back. Resentful as I was, I refused to take his advice. A week later, the windmill painting had gone. I think I feel more guilty than the criminals who had stolen these works of art from us. And now I wonder whether the Palestinians who fled during the so-called "war of independence" and the 6 Day war and so on, and who are forced to flee now, owing to the continuing destruction of their villages, whether they feel guilty, guilty that the Arabs have lost every war, and ashamed to find themselves in the concentration camp that Gaza is, or in the concentration camps that the so-called refugee camps are in the Lebanon. And of course I wonder about Esau. How did he feel about agreeing to let his birth right be taken by his smooth-talking brother, in return for that mess of pottage? I am willing to bet he felt guilty about that. Better, surely, to retell the story, from a Palestinian point-of-view. Esau arrives at Jacob's door. He has been hunting all week. But there has been no game and the hunt has been thankless. Esau is desperately hungry now, and so he asks his brother for something to eat. And his brother, says, yes, I will give you to eat: a mess of pottage – in return for your birth-right. And Esau says, you're pulling my leg.

When I wake up how do I know who I was when I went to sleep? I don't. I don't know. Any more than I can know that I am descended from Adam and Eve. Or perhaps I'm descended from the Lady of the Sun, who was stolen by those eagles. I awake intact. And that is all I can assume. I could be Uncle Hermon in Cologne. He was a Jew who had actually returned to Germany after the war, charged with overseeing German reparation for the six million. I loved my Uncle Hermon. Balding, like the rest of my uncles, but less solemn, not quite as stately, and always looking up with a smile. It was in Cologne that I bought Poncho Pup. The first of my glove puppets. He was a Steiff puppet with an honest, earnest expression, made of that lovely Steiff material that masqueraded as fur. Uncle Hermon helped me set up a little stage, and I began performing puppet shows for him. After that, I became a collector of puppets. Wherever my mother and I went on holiday, I scoured the shops for puppets, and I ended up with a troupe of about seventy, all of them glove puppets, just as Poncho was, with representatives in the company from all over the world. Pongo Pup was the director, the director of the Peargrove Puppet Theatre, named after our cottage in Pearman's Grove. Later I procured a professional Punch-and-Judy Theatre, which I would set up in homes for the mentally and physically impaired who would try hard to applaud the antics of my puppets. Really that was all down to my Uncle Hermon. Of course I do realise now that my family was to a considerable degree responsible for the Zionist funding of Israel. But during the first ten years of my life, growing up as a boy with a widowed mother, these were the uncles whose visits I enjoyed and who I did enjoy visiting. There was no father for me, as there was no father for my Uncle Paul. Uncles were the only men I knew. All of them balding, and with high foreheads. On one occasion, my Uncle Felix, the Israeli statesman, came to Upshire where my mother was living with her mother (I never realised that these uncles were "great"). I can't have been much more than three years old. I remember we went for a walk in an autumnal Epping Forest, and that Uncle Felix hushed me as we looked down from a leaf-strewn ridge. Then a herd of deer passed by, silently, under the branches below us. I also remember visiting my Jewish grandparents in New York. It was there that I had my fourth birthday. My grandfather Martin took me for a walk by the Hudson. I was playing with a rubber ball. I threw it and it bounced and bounced, and then it rolled to the embankment's edge and fell into the river. Silently my grandfather and I watched the ball floating further and further away. Remember, my father, his son, died in the last few weeks of the war, serving in

Naples, before I was born. The ball grew distant as it floated downstream and then at last it disappeared. I felt we shared its loss. By then my grandfather was directing Zionist funding from New York. His career had begun far earlier, in Berlin, starting with the creation of the Keren haYesod, an early fund-raising organisation. This he ran in Germany from 1920 to 1923. From December 1923, through January 1925, he directed the Keren haYesod activities in Austria.